The
CITY
Beyond
PLAY

PHILIP JOSÉ
FARMER
AND
DANNY ADAMS

Introduction by CHRIS ROBERSON
Afterword by TRACY KNIGHT

The
CITY
Beyond
PLAY

PS Publishing 2007

Published in September 2007 by PS Publishing Ltd. by
arrangement with the author. All rights reserved by the author.

FIRST EDITION

ISBN
978-1-905834-90-7 (Deluxe slipcased hardcover)
978-1-905834-25-9 (Jacketed hardcover)
978-1-905834-24-2 (Trade hardcover)

Design and layout by Alligator Tree Graphics

Printed and bound in Great Britain by Biddles Ltd

PS Publishing Ltd
Grosvenor House / 1 New Road
Hornsea, HU18 1PG / Great Britain

e-mail: editor@pspublishing.co.uk
Internet: http://www.pspublishing.co.uk

$\mathcal{A}$ GRAND $\mathcal{A}$DVENTURE

Chris Roberson

*I*N 1970, PHILIP JOSÉ FARMER BEGAN WORK ON A NOVELLA. Entitled *The City Beyond Play*, it was about historical recreationists in a post-scarcity future, a fugitive on the run, and things never being quite what they seemed. Having outlined the plot and written the first few chapters, though, Phil set it aside unfinished and moved on to other projects.

Thereby hangs the tale . . .

BY 1970, PHILIP JOSÉ FARMER HAD TWENTY-THREE BOOKS IN print, five of them released in that year *alone*. He'd already published the first several installments in his World of Tiers series, the first of his John Carmody novels, his first works of pulp revival—including the incomparable *A Feast Unknown,* its sequels *Lord of the Trees* and *The Mad Goblin,* and the somewhat more serious examination of the "feral man" trope, *Lord Tyger*—and the first installment of his Riverworld sequence as a serialized novel in *Worlds of If.* He'd been nominated for the Hugo Award five times, winning twice, once for Most Promising New Talent, and once for Best Novella with "Riders of the Purple Wage," which also garnered a Nebula Award nomination.

In 1946, at the age of twenty-eight, Phil had made his first sale, a non-SF story called "O'Brien and Obrenov," to the hallowed pulp, *Adventure.* He'd been an avid reader of pulp magazines as a child, so there's some fitting justice that his debut would come in the pages of one of the earliest, best, and longest-running of the pulps. A few years later, Phil would burst onto the SF scene, daring tradition and convention with stories like "The Lovers" and "Mother," breaking new ground throughout his long career, but he never forgot his pulp roots. In his most prolific years, he revisited the fictional worlds of his childhood, those of Tarzan (*A Feast Unknown, Tarzan Alive, Lord Tyger, Lord of the Trees, The Dark Heart of Time*), Doc Savage (*Doc Savage: His Apocalyptic Life, The Mad Goblin, Escape from Loki*), Jules Verne (*The Other Log of Phileas Fogg*), L. Frank Baum (*A Barnstormer of Oz*), Arthur Conan Doyle (*The Adventure of the Peerless Peer*), H. Rider Haggard (*Hadon of Ancient Opar*), and many others. His most successful works, it can be argued, are those in which he manages to capture the frisson of adventure and imagination he must have felt as a young reader first visiting these fictional worlds, but in new worlds of his own imagining, with horizon-expanding scientific notions and stylistic sophistication—the World of Tiers, Riverworld, Day-world—settings to which he would return again and again.

And, just as the worlds of Burroughs and Robeson and Doyle had influenced a young Phil Farmer, so did Phil's worlds influence a new generation of readers and writers, among them me and Danny Adams.

I WAS BORN IN 1970, AND FOR MOST OF MY LIFE I'VE LABORED IN Phil's shadow.

I wanted to be a writer before I'd ever read a book of Phil's, but in him I found a model for the *type* of writer I'd become. I dedicated my small press novel *Cybermancy Incorporated* to Phil (which recounted the adventures of Jon Bonaventure *Carmody*), and one of my proudest moments as a publisher was the release of *Myths for the Modern Age: Philip José Farmer's Wold Newton Universe*, edited by Win Scott Eckert.

I'm not sure when I first read one of his books, but I couldn't have been much older than ten or eleven when I picked up his *Doc Savage: His Apocalyptic Life* at a second-hand bookstore. By the time I was in high school I'd already worked my way through worlds of rivers, and of tiers, and of days, and was hungry for more. By the time I graduated from college I'd read everything of Phil's that the University of Texas library system had in its stacks, which must have been nearly everything he'd published, including articles in obscure mimeographed fanzines devoted to writers like Edgar Rice Burroughs. I remember in particular studying the story collection *The Grand Adventure* with the intensity of a Talmudic scholar, and I still think that "After King Kong Fell" is one of the best stories I've ever read.

When I was thirty-four, the same age Phil had been when he sold his first science fiction story, "The Lovers," to *Startling Stories*, I was a finalist for the John W. Campbell Award for Best New Writer, named after the noted editor of *Astounding Stories* who, when he rejected "The Lovers," reportedly said that the story had nauseated him. When Phil was thirty-five, he won the Hugo Award for Most Promising New Talent, precursor to the Campbell Award, primarily on the strength of that story.

The key lessons I learned from a careful study of Phil's work were that big ideas and a sense of adventure need not be mutually exclusive, that there's nothing wrong with a writer having fun, and the importance of never forgetting one's influences.

DANNY ADAMS, CLEARLY, HAS LEARNED THOSE LESSONS, TOO.

Like me, Danny was born in 1970. We've never met, but he had a childhood I can only imagine, and envy deeply. When he was eleven, right around the time that I picked up *Doc Savage: His Apocalyptic Life*, Danny read a book written by his grandmother's brother-in-law, the man he knew as "Uncle Phil." It was *To Your Scattered Bodies Go*, and it changed Danny's life, in much the same way that it would change mine a short time later. But our experiences differ in that Danny, when he finished the book and had questions about it, could call up his Uncle Phil and get the answers. While I read and reread every scrap of story written by Phil I could get my hands on, trying to learn how to become a writer, Danny took family trips to Peoria, to visit the great man in his home, and got writing advice directly from the source.

By 2005, Danny was starting to build a reputation as a talented new writer, with story sales to online venues and small press magazines. He'd written a novel, and after sending the first few chapters to his Uncle Phil to critique, it was decided that he would be allowed to complete the novella *The City Beyond Play*, left unfinished since the year Danny was born, working from Phil's original outline.

At the time of this writing, with the novella completed and set to be published, Danny (like me) is thirty-five, the same age Phil had been when he won the Shasta prize novel contest for his submission, *I Owe for the Flesh*, which he would later rework as *To Your Scattered Bodies Go*, the first of his Riverworld series, the book that set Danny on the writer's path in the first place.

THERE ARE SYMMETRIES AND COINCIDENCES THAT SEEM TO LINK me to Danny, and both of us to Phil. But what of the novella itself? What of *The City Beyond Play*?

It is the story I never knew we were missing, but which I'm delighted has been found. Vintage Philip José Farmer, it possesses a quick tempo, clever ideas, adventure, and humor, but with an added flavor that can only be attributed to his collaborator, Danny Adams. Danny has risen to the daunting challenge of finishing a work begun by a master of the genre at the height of his powers, a task I'm not sure I'd have had the nerve to tackle. And he's performed admirably, the result so splendidly seamless that I'm not certain where Phil's words leave off and Danny's begin.

In *The City Beyond Play* can be found all the lessons I learned from Phil's novels, and which Danny, too, has taken to heart. It is a true collaboration, between a master craftsman and a talented journeyman. It is, in short, a grand adventure, and one I feel privileged to have been able to share.

Chris Roberson
Austin, Texas
April 2006

The
CITY
Beyond
PLAY

"*H*ALT, KNAVE!"

The young man stopped. He was tall, well built, handsome, and had dark blue eyes and long rich yellow hair. He wore a flat square blue velveteen cap with a tiny red feather, a sequined yellow jacket with huge puffed sleeves and a deep V-neckline exposing a thickly muscled chest, green-white-and-red checked tights with an orange codpiece, and blue calf-length boots with turned-up toes. His broad leather silver-studded belt supported a dagger in its sheath.

He looked ill at ease, as if he were not used to the clothes or indeed anything in his environment.

Behind him was the narrow dirt road down which he had walked for an hour. It rose gradually, winding among the bright green meadows and now and then lost in the thick stands of trees. Its brown line was visible for miles on the hills until it merged with the blue of the sky.

Before him was a twenty foot wide brook. Its clear water revealed that it was deep enough for trout and other fish but shallow enough to be forded.

On the stream's opposite shore, resplendent on a huge black horse, was an armored knight. His crest was a golden dragon, and his triangular shield bore a golden background with a red bar in its middle and on the bar three azure beer steins capped with white foam.

The armored man pointed a long spear with a knob of some silvery looking metal at its tip. Behind him was a forest of redwood and pines.

"Well, knave, what is your name?" the deep voice behind the lowered visor said.

"I am not a knave," the young man said.

Far overhead the golden delta of an airliner cut the blue.

"I don't mean you're a villain, though you may be a villein," the man said. "Speak up, and fairly, before I chastise thee for disrespect."

"Who are you?" the young man said.

The voice behind the visor bellowed, "Know you not, greenhorn, that I hight Sir Bobaunce of High Tower? Did they not inform thee at the border that you are in my territory? Did they not inform thee that I am in dire need of a stableboy?"

"That they did, certes," the young man said. He grimaced at his involuntary and ready falling into an archaic manner of speech. Pseudoarchaic, rather. If he was addressed as *thee* in the objective case, why not *thou* in the nominative?

"What is your name, knave? Speak, or I give thee such a buffet with the hard end of my lance, that . . . "

"Wilson Gore, and it please your highness."

"It does not please me. And I remind thee, knave, which term is, by the way, a term for boy, not a wicked so-and-so, since it has reverted to its original meaning, that you best keep a civil tongue in your head. When you were admitted into Scadia, you swore to observe our laws and customs. So you will address me from here on out, or in, as the case may be, as sir or sire or your knightship. Since I am lord of High Tower, you will not be reprimanded if you address me as your lordship. But highness, no. Not unless I win the kingship, which I am rather likely to do at this next tourney at Camelot."

Wilson Gore said, "Yes, your knightship."

He looked up at the sky again. The airliner was gone, and nothing remained to indicate that he was still in the 22nd century A.D.

At Sir Bobaunce's orders, he followed along behind the horse. After a few minutes, the knight slowed to allow Gore to keep up with him. He raised his visor and revealed an aquiline but good-looking face. He looked as if he were about thirty-five. His hair was black, and his moustache was thick and drooping.

However, his chin did sag with fat, and the curve of armor suggested that it was making room for a robin-red-breast's paunch underneath.

Sir Bobaunce stopped the horse under a huge redwood, unhooked a bottle from the saddle, uncapped it, and drank long from it. Then he winked at Gore and passed the bottle down to him. Gore drank, smacked his lips, and drank again. The bourbon was superb and cold to boot.

"Here, don't gulp it all, knave," the knight said, and he snatched the bottle away and emptied it. He started the horse to walking again and burst into a song. Its words and sentiment were medieval, but the tune was certainly from Gilbert and Sullivan. The overture to *The Mikado*, if Gore remembered correctly.

A mile and a half of winding path through heavy woods brought them into the clear. Ahead was a gentle slope on top of which was a pretty little village of thatched cottages. Beyond and above it, on a rugged hill, was a tall thin castle with two slender towers and many flags flying.

"So it's really all true," Gore said.

"What say, knave?" Sir Bobaunce looked down at him with eyes that had become very red.

"I've read about this place and seen some fidos which talked about it. But there's very little known about it, since you people have forbidden publicity. I knew it was true, but I still couldn't believe it. But here it is, just as they said."

"The less said about what lies on yonder side of the thorn forest, the better," the knight growled. "We don't care to talk about it here, Will Son of Gore. Yonder 'tis a land overrun with dragons, mantichoras, wizards, witches, and various monsters and ogres. A wasteland it is, evil, of no good intent and incapable of being put to good use. So do not discuss it with anyone, knave, unless someone of quality requires thee to open your mouth about it."

Gore did not reply, though he had to clamp his lips to keep from doing so. He had been told at the border station about the schizophrenic state of mind of the Scadians. And he had been told that he must not argue about their concept of reality, since it was his desire to enter as a citizen-on-probation.

Wilson Gore was a murderer, but he was intelligent, as murderers often are. He would conform, because he must disappear into the citizenry, be one of them, and so be safe. But there would be much that would rile him, and he must watch himself closely. Besides, whatever drawbacks this country had, it did offer rapid advancement for a man with ambition and ability.

Sir Bobaunce reined in his horse. "Lord and master of all I survey," he said. "I own the castle and yon village of Briarwood and the souls therein and the cattle and the woods roundabout. Four square miles acknowledge me as suzerain."

"Very impressive."

"Very impressive what, knave?"

"Your knightship, sire."

"That's better, my knave. You were told, of course, that if you fail, out you go, out beyond the great thorn forest, into the deadly desert and the wasteland? God have mercy on your soul if you are driven from this fair land into that howling and deadly nihilum."

Gore had also been told that nobody had ever returned through the border station into the Outside.

"You mean everybody likes it so much they stay?" Gore had asked the station inspector. "That's incredible. But it also explains why the outside knows so little about Scadia."

"I didn't say everybody loved it," the inspector had said. "What I said was that nobody has ever returned. There's more than one way to stay here, you know."

The village had looked picturesque with its peaked roofs, white plaster walls painted with colorful murals, and green stone chimneys. At close range, it kept its charm. The street was unpaved, but everything was clean. The villagers were clean and their clothing was new-appearing and many-colored. The women wore skirts that reached to the ground but made up for this with deep-scoop necklines. The few children were naked and healthy-looking. The only animals were some dogs and cats and pet birds: canaries and parrots.

The women curtsied and the men touched their foreheads as Sir Bobaunce passed them. He responded with a wave of his gauntleted hand.

Gore commented on the cleanliness.

The knight leaned over, though not too far, since he did not want to be brought crashing to the ground by the weight of his armor. He slapped Gore hard on the back with his mailed hand, knocking him down.

Roaring, Gore jumped up, but he stopped when the knight brought the knobbed end of his lance around as if to whack him with it.

"Now, knave, I bare thee no ill will. But you must start learning, and a dog remembers a whipping. Do not speak to your betters unless spoken to. Unless a great emergency demands otherwise, of course. Now, to answer your question, since it is something you should know.

"Yes, the medieval villages were stinking pigsties. And so were the castles of the lords. But we have recreated the Middles Ages, *not as they were but as they should have been.*

"Don't ever forget that."

Gore knew that, since he had read the history of the society that built this community. He did not, however, believe that a hard blow on a man's spine was an anachronism to be desired. He determined to pay the knight back the first chance he got to do so without fear of being punished. And Sir Bobaunce would get more than just a fist between his shoulders.

The dirt road wound up and around the hill, ending at the only castle entrance, which faced the village. The moat circling the castle was about forty feet across and was, the knight assured him, thirty feet deep.

Some large and peculiar-looking reptiles rested on several small mud islands. Bobaunce referred to them as his "dwarf" dragon pets", but Gore knew they were descended from crocodiles mutated in the genetic laboratories about a hundred years ago. They were thirty feet long and sprouted tall reddish crests along their backs. Their legs were much longer and their jaws much shorter than those of their unmutated ancestors.

"Beastly amount of meat goes to feed those beasts," the knight said. "But they do discourage swimmers. Every swimmer means that much less beef I have to feed the beasts, haw, haw!"

Wilson Gore opened his mouth and then closed it.

Sir Bobaunce, seeing his expression, said, "Speak up, knave!"

"Your knightship, why would anybody want to swim in the moat?"

"A good question, knave. Why, indeed! Well, for one thing, to gain the secret entrance to my keep. There is one in every keep, though the Wicked Duke and the Witch of Agravaine do not play according to the rules. But then what can one expect from those thorough rotters?

"So my enemies every now and then send in a swimmer, some squire hoping to earn his knighthood, or some young knight hoping to earn a heroic reputation. They dive under the water and search all along the base of the wall for a hidden entrance. But all they find is egress, by way of entrance into the bellies of my pets, haw, haw!

"However," and Sir Bobaunce sobered, "there is another reason why men strive to get into my keep. You will see her in a few minutes."

Sir Bobaunce stopped the horse by a wooden pole with a hook from which hung a slender bugle. The knight blew several bars on it, which Gore recognized as from the overture to *The Pirates of Penzance*. Immediately, several heads appeared above the crenellations of the towers flanking the entrance.

"Lazy varlets! Sleeping again!" the knight bellowed. "Damn your eyes, lower the drawbridge, raise the portcullis! Why didn't you see me coming a long time ago and have the way open for your lord and master?"

"'A must remind your knightship," a thin voice said, "that his self told us to keep the castle shut until his self blew the code-signal. Your knightship said that some enemy might dress up in his armor, and . . . "

"I know what I said, knave!" the knight bellowed. "If I want a lecture, I'll ask for it! Quickly! Down with the bridge and up with the cullis! What I tell thee once is true!"

A few minutes later, the horse cantered on across the drawbridge and into the courtyard. Gore followed and watched as two youths helped the knight off the horse and removed his helmet and gauntlets. His black hair was cut short, as if a bowl had been placed on it before the shears attacked.

The squires removed the rest of the armor, and Sir Bobaunce scratched various places and flexed his knees several times. He was about six foot one inch tall, broad-shouldered, deep-chested, and large-paunched. He wore a scarlet shirt with balloon sleeves and Kelly green tights.

One of the youths brought a chair for him to sit down on while calf-length canary yellow boots were put on him. A third juvenile, a lovely blonde, appeared with a silvery tray on which was a great stein of beer.

Sir Bobaunce said, "Thankee, wench," and drained what must have been a quart and a half without putting the stein down. Thereafter, he belched so loudly that the courtyard walls seemed to echo.

The knight waved at the stranger.

"This be Will's son of Gore, our new stableboy. You, Alain, take him to the horses and teach him his duties. It might be that he is somewhat hard of learning."

Alain, tall, thick-limbed, red-haired, and long-chinned, smirked.

He said, "The knave looks quite capable, to the manure born, if his lordship doesn't mind me saying so."

"Haw, haw, very good!" the knight said. "I'll have to remember that! Now, where is M'lady?"

"M'lady has been informed that M'lord is here," Alain said. "I don't know what's holding M'lady up, sire."

"Hmm," Sir Bobaunce said. "Well, I suppose I must go to her then."

He muttered, "Sulking again, I suppose."

A woman stepped out from the shadowy archway into the courtyard, and Wilson Gore knew what the knight had meant when he said there was another reason for swimmers to dare the moat.

For her, he would have tackled the crocodiles bare handed.

M'LADY MELISOUNDE WAS A TALL WOMAN WITH LONG honey-colored hair and large gray eyes. She was somewhere between twenty-five and twenty-eight. To Wilson Gore, she was the most beautiful woman in the world. The first sight of her hit him in the stomach, and the blow became an ache which spread to his chest.

"Yes," Sir Bobaunce drawled, stroking his moustache. "She is the most radiant of visions. I have killed men for her and shall have to do so again. Now, knave, a cat may look at a queen without rebuke. But a stableboy should keep the naked lust from his face. I do not blame you, but I do not want to see such an expression again. If I do, I shall kick you out of the castle, and then God help you."

Gore said nothing. He started to turn towards Alain, but, seeing Melisounde walking towards her husband, could not resist another look.

She was lovely indeed as she walked, swayed like a tree in a breeze, rather. Then she was embracing the big oaf, her husband, and kissing him. And the vulgar swine was patting her lovely rounded buttock in public.

"I've missed thee very much, my honeypot," she said in a voice to match the beauty of her face. Or so it seemed to Gore.

"And I thou," Sir Bobaunce said, permitting himself even more familiarities.

"Boor!" Gore muttered.

"Careful, stableboy," Alain said, grinning. "Or his knightship will cuff thee so heartily thy ears will ring vespers through high noon."

"Thou must needs come now, and we'll have a love feast to celebrate thy return," Melisounde said, withdrawing from his embrace.

"He's only been gone three hours," Alain said. "Whew! What a woman!"

Gore made a mental linguistic note. *Thou* was reserved for family usage or among equals. *You* was used when a noble addressed an inferior. *Thou* and *thee* could be used among equals, or near-equals, in the lower classes.

Classes, however, did not mean in Scadia what it meant in the Middle Ages. Theoretically, everyone here, no matter who his parents were, had a chance to work up to king or queen. Or, even better, a duke or duchess. A king ruled for only one year at a time. He could not succeed himself. And after he had been king three times, he became a duke and remained one.

Gore was suddenly recalled to his immediate surroundings with a boot in the rear.

Cursing, he turned on Alain with his fists. He became silent when he saw his knightship grinning. Then the beefy fellow, his arm around his wife's slim waist, his hand on her curving hip, walked away. Apparently, Alain was to take care of whatever disciplinary problems arose.

Alain said, "I took plenty of kicks when I was a stableboy, and I took them with a smile and a thankee. I'm a better man for them. So will thou be, if thou want to do thy duties properly. So far, you've been treated with more toleration and downright forbearance than is ever given a native-born. We will make some allowances for the ignorant immigrant. But not many."

Gore breathed deeply and unclenched his hands. He could not afford to get kicked out of Scadia. But Alain would get his some day. The hard way.

He followed Alain into the stables, which were housed in the castle proper just past the left portcullis tower. They held stalls for forty horses, although there were only twenty animals therein. Alain showed Gore where he could bed down on the straw in one of the stalls.

Gore had seen horses many times on the fido. Horse operas were as popular as ever; *Gunsmoke* and *Wagon Train* were popular among American history reenactors. He had also seen wild horses at a distance in a National Park, and he had been close to tame ones in the zoo. But standing next to these huge, powerfully muscled, hard-hooved, big-toothed, wild-eyed, and nervous beasts was not the same as observing them on the fido or through bars. And to be expected to wash them, curry them, rub elbows with them, as it were, was to expect too much from a civilized man.

"There are thy tools," Alain said, gesturing at the bucket and various brushes and combs. "Have the brutes washed and curried by suppertime."

"By *supper*time?"

"Thou must not react to an order with an outraged face. By suppertime. Else no supper for thee. I had to do thus, and, if I'd failed, I would not today be Sir Bobaunce's senior squire. So get thou to sweating until thou stink like a horse, knave."

Gore clamped down on his retort and set to work.

He was not nearly done when the supper bell rang. But when he finished he discovered that he would not have to go without supper, despite what Alain said. He just would not be allowed to eat with the help in the kitchen. That, he told himself, was all to the good. He didn't want to eat with the swine, anyway.

However, he did eat with the swine. The stockyards were next to the stable. A few pigs were kept there for butchering, and the kitchen maid who gave him a plate told him he must eat from it in the sty.

"Alain says he was told thou weren't fit to eat with the hogs," she said, grinning. "But he has taken a shine to thee, and he defended thee, saying thou *were* fit to eat with them."

Gore did not reply. He went into the big shadowy room and sat down in a corner. He had been told that pigs stink abominably, but the sty, though it had a wallow, emitted only a very faint odor. It was not nearly as pleasant as the odors of horses or manure, but it was endurable. He was so hungry after his hard work that he ate everything on the plate. And though the enormous, wicked-looking, evil-eyed sow came over to the fence and glared at him, he did not stop eating. He feared the pigs even more than the horses, but at least he was not ordered to get into the wallow with them.

The steak, potatoes, tomatoes, onions, and bread and butter tasted better than anything he had ever had except when he was visiting the National Parks. These foods were home-grown, not duplicated by energy-matter transformers in the great factories outside the multileveled cities. There was loving care in their every molecule and a large amount of natural fertilizer.

However, if he had not been so hungry, he might not have cared so much for the food. It did feature a certain rankness, an over-richness, which his palate would have to learn to love. But it would do so. It would do so.

He was going to acquire a taste for everything in this valley. He must.

Especially, he was going to acquire Melisounde. He had the taste for her. There remained only the means of getting her.

He dreamed of her that night. Later, he dreamed that a horse was trampling him, and he awoke shaking with horror. He had no trouble getting back to sleep, however, and he would have slept past dawn if Alain had not rapped the soles of his bare feet with a stick.

He came up out of the straw cursing, only to receive a bucketful of cold water in the face.

"Thy bath, my lord of the horse manure," Alain said, dancing back to avoid Gore's blind swings.

"How does anyone here survive?" Gore said after stopping his rushes at Alain and wiping away the water. "I'd think everybody would be out to kill everybody else."

"Thou're taking the kicks now, but the time will come, an thou prove thyself, when thou'll be doing the kicking. Thou can forgive much when thou'rt on the giving end of a hard boot."

Gore made a face, but he obeyed the orders to shovel out the manure, which would go to the fields, and put clean straw in the stables. Then he showered—modern plumbing was allowed in Scadia—and went to a late breakfast. But he was sent away with his plate again, though this time he ate in the stables. The flies annoyed him by buzzing around his head and landing on his food. The original species of horsefly was extinct, but the housefly had filled the ecological niche.

Gore had just finished eating when Alain told him to saddle ten horses. Quickly. His knightship had decided to go hunting earlier than planned.

Gore grumbled that he had not known anything about Sir Bobaunce's plans in the first place. But he hastened to obey before Alain's leather toe caught him in the rear. However, Alain had to assist him, since Wilson had not the slightest knowledge of how to saddle a horse.

While they worked, the dogs were released from the kennels across the courtyard. Their barking made the yard a well of hideous noise.

Presently Sir Bobaunce and Lady Melisounde entered the courtyard, followed by a score of lords and ladies. The knight was dressed in leather riding clothes brilliant enough to have scared off half the deer in the land. He wore a broad black beret with a great red-dyed ostrich plume. He gripped the handle of an enormous beer stein of carved granite. Before mounting, he emptied the stein. Alain then handed him up another, which the knight emptied before riding out.

Gore was busy helping various guests mount their steeds. Apparently, these had been staying in the castle for a week; he had known nothing about them because no one had thought to tell him. And they had not told him because it was none of his business; he did not matter.

Despite having to work so hard, Wilson caught many views of M'lady Melisounde. She wore a green velvet triangular cap with a red plume, a high-necked beige jacket with ballooning sleeves, an ankle-length split skirt with green and white checks, and scarlet boots. She rode side-saddle, and she looked to Gore as if she should be a queen, not just the wife of a small-holding knight.

He was so entranced watching her that he failed to get out of the way of a guest's horse. He was knocked forward onto the ground and had to roll quickly to one side to avoid being trampled. Everybody, including Melisounde, laughed. He was up quickly and then dodged behind a nervously dancing horse to avoid Alain's riding crop.

Sir Bobaunce called out sharply, and Alain put the crop down.

"Get thyself a horse and follow us," Alain said to Wilson. "His knight-ship wants thee to meet us at the Black Tor with liquid refreshments. His knightship gets mighty impatient when he is out of beer and booze, so thou had better be there."

"Yes, but where . . . ?"

One of the guests, a black man, apparently master of the hunt, blew on his bugle. The dogs were unleashed, and they leaped barking and yapping out through the portcullis mainway and across the drawbridge. Then the lord of the castle, yelling, "Yoicks! Go get 'em!" and some exceedingly coarse injunctions, rode out. The others followed, leaving Wilson Gore wondering where the liquid refreshments were kept and where the Black Tor was.

SOME OF THE SERVANTS LIVED IN THE CASTLE, BUT MOST LIVED
in the village of Briarwood. Wilson did not know why anybody
would want to be a servant if he could be a lord. Outside—he had started
to think of everything extra-Scadia as the great Outside—nobody had to
work if they did not care to do so. In the economy of abundance, established over one hundred and fifty years ago, the minimum guaranteed
income had a very high floor indeed. Most wealthy people of the mid-
20th century would have been quite happy with the material things given
free to all in the 22nd century.

They would not, however, have liked the restrictions on travel outside
their cities and restrictions on conspicuous consumption. Nor would they
have liked it that the only way to gain prestige was to be an artist or a
scientist or a servant of the public. A "servant of the public" could be
anything from a waitress in a Folk Restaurant or a plumber or an electronic repairman through a school teacher or medical doctor to the mayor
of Manhattan or the president of the North American Commonwealth.
"Servant" had different connotations and denotations in the 22nd
century. It was usually associated with prestige.

But in Scadia, it indicated a person who was content to wait on the
upper classes, content to be without ambition, content to remain lower
class.

The truth seemed to be that, just as there were born leaders and
followers, so there were born masters and servants.

The difference between the Middle Ages, most ages, in fact, and Scadian times was that the servantship was voluntary. A man could work his way up to a lordship, and many had. But if a man was happy with his station as farmer or servant, he had no pressure put on him to leave his happy state for the sake of prestige or ambition. Moreover, the lower classes were not harassed or put to the sword or their possessions burned or stolen and their women raped during wartime.

They might find themselves with a new lord one morning. But the change meant little to the farmers or servants. Their rights and obligations were the same. They would not be exploited or oppressed.

Gore, standing in the middle of the suddenly quiet courtyard, wondered if he shouldn't change his plans. Why try to lose himself in the high when he could do it so much more easily among the low?

All he had to do was declare for servantship, live in the village, perform his non-onerous duties there or in the castle, and have plenty of leisure time to enjoy himself. He could marry a village girl—they were all good-looking and cheerful—and settle down. It was true that the low classes afforded fewer people among whom to hide. Here, unlike all previous societies, the lower classes were greatly outnumbered by the higher.

But then any police searching for him would look in the aristocracy for him. Knowing his psych index, they would know that he would not be content to be a servant. The police would not even bother looking among the lowly.

That was what he would do! Make himself suffer a strange sea-change! Show that he was the master of his own character, which was the same thing as his own fate, and double back on the psychic track. He would become a Proteus of the personality. He would never be found.

A few minutes later he told himself: To hell with that! He did not want to be on the receiving end. He wanted to dish it out from the seat of the mighty.

Besides—and this was the determining reason, or, at least, his greatest rationalization—if he remained a servant, he could never have Melisounde.

"Where is the Black Tor?" he asked Jack Ratch, a villager who kept bees and provided the castle with honey and mead. "And what is the Black Tor?"

"'Tis a tall crooked blackish rock about two miles to the northwest o' here, knave," Jack Ratch said. "It lies in a corner o' the land o' Sir Palamides the Saracen. Sir Palamides, if thou did not notice, was the master o' the hunt and a guest. He . . . "

"How do I get there? And don't call me knave, old man."

Jack raised thick white eyebrows. "Why not? Ain't thou?"

"Not to thee, a villager. Nor to anyone for long."

"Perhaps they will name thee Sir Orgulous when thou gain thy knighthood, if ever thou do," Jack Ratch said. "Sir Orgulous de Payne en-le-Cul will be thy full name." He cackled.

"I know not what the hell thou mean," Gore said. "And I won't inquire, since I don't wish to mix it up with the lowborn. Now, where do I get Sir Bobaunce's drinks?"

"'Tis no business of mine. I'm the honeyman." Ratch turned away.

Gore spun him back around. "Don't turn your back on me, old man!"

Ratch blinked but did not shrink away. He said, "If you would climb, you should get a sturdy ladder. And you can't trust the rounds if you've been abusing them."

"Meaning that I should kowtow to the likes of you?"

"You're a stranger and alone, and you need others to teach you."

Gore released Ratch, swallowed, smiled—though it came hard—and held out his hand.

"I apologize for losing my temper. No hard feelings?"

"None, knave."

Ratch shook his hand. The old man had a grip that a 25-year-old would have been proud of.

"Knave it shall be then," Gore told him. "But one day . . . "

"See the butler about his knightship's refreshments," Ratch said, and he walked away.

Gore asked several of the household help where he could find the butler. His polite requests finally got him directions to the dungeon. This was, essentially, the basement and consisted of the enormous booze and wine cellar, a few cells for prisoners which had apparently never been used, and a number of dimly lit moisture-oozing corridors leading to dark places somewhere in the bowels of the castle.

The butler, James o' the Inkwell, was standing under the flickering light of a torch set in a stand on the wall. The tall thin long-faced man was inventorying barrels, tuns, casks, and racks of wine bottles. At least he seemed to be busy listing them, though he may have heard Gore coming and so put on the appearance of activity. Several newly emptied wine bottles were sitting on a nearby table. The butler's breath was strong with very good vintage.

"Sho, thou'rt the new knave from the washtelands?" He leaned back and forth as if he were a buoy on a gentle sea.

"Yes, that be I," Gore said, determined not to take offense or, at least, not to show that he had. "His knightship told me to bring the wine and booze for the hunting party to the Black Tor."

"Which thou had better do quickly or pay for thy indolence and ineptness," James o' the Inkwell said.

"I hope there's something left here for me to take to his knightship." He regretted the words as soon as they were spoken. But there they were.

"Stableboy! Would *thou* mock me, the butler, a lowly fellow who is, no matter what one says to the contrary, fit to . . ."

"Eat with the hogs," Gore said. "I know."

"That is all thou know."

"Just give me the stuff for his Boozeship, and I'll be on my way."

The butler laughed loudly and long. In between brays, he gasped, "His Boozeship! That's a good one!"

Finally, over his fits of merriment, the butler picked various bottles and packed them in a big wicker case stuffed with straw.

"Here be the 2069 wine, from an excellent wet year, which is wasted on his Boozeship, haw, haw! That honorable swine is a guzzler, and a mighty one, I'll say that for him. When he's sober, he has an excellent discrimination, a tender palate. Unfortunately, he's never long sober, and so great wines and liquor, or even good stuff, is wasted on him. 'Tis enough to drive even a second-rate connoisseur to drink, and I am a first-rate one, if not a great one."

Gore hoisted the basket onto his back by its strap. The basket and contents seemed to weigh about seventy-five pounds.

"If thou go through the woods, be careful, knave!" the butler shouted after him. "Beware of the Green Baron! I hear he is skulking in this neighborhood, or so the last report from the king's high sheriff said!"

Gore almost stopped to ask what he meant, but decided he should not waste any time. He had not the least idea of how soon the hunters would be at the Black Tor, and he did not want to get there and find them thirsty and in a bad humor.

A few minutes later, saddle packed, he mounted a big brown stallion. The beast must have smelled the molecules of apprehension pouring from its rider's sweat glands. It acted exactly as it wished, which was in every way contrary to Gore's desires.

The horse danced sideways through the village's only street while the citizens and their children laughed so hard they rolled in the dust. Gore was hot with embarrassment and cold with fear but also thankful that the horse had not leaped off the drawbridge into the moat, as he had thought it would as they galloped along the edge of the bridge.

Then the big brute scraped his leg against the corner of a house, and he forgot any gratitude that might have survived the jeering of the villagers.

He shouted and pulled on the reins and kicked the beast in the ribs with his heels. But the animal seemed to enjoy his efforts to control it. It turned its head and snickered at him.

When the two had gotten, somehow, through the village and were headed towards the woods, but in a direction opposite that in which they were supposed to be going, Gore got off.

He did not, however, just abandon ship. He hung on to the reins and managed to stop the beast. Then, while it wheeled, dragging him around and around, or backed, still dragging him, he got the wicker case unstrapped from the saddle. It slid off and would have struck the earth hard if he had not succeeded in placing his body between it and the ground. Its heavy butt drove into his stomach and knocked the air out, and he toppled with a crash. The stallion galloped away and was soon out of sight.

Gore hoped it would stay out of sight.

When he had regained his breath and quit shaking, he got up. He hoisted the case to his back and started into the woods in what he hoped was the proper direction. Actually, he anticipated getting to the Black Tor on foot faster than he would have on the horse, even if it had been well-behaved. According to the servants, the road ran around the edge of the woods to the great rock. By going as the crow flies, or the pedestrian trudges, he could cut three miles off his journey. But he would be in a forest so dense that only a man on foot could make it. A horse would not be able to force its way through the bushes.

"This land is made to seem much bigger than it actually is by cunningly placed growths of extremely thick woods," the border inspector had told him. "The many woods force one to go around to get to one's destination. Time is usually of little consequence here, but the feeling of spaciousness is. Hence, the lack of direct routes."

Sweating, even though the towering redwoods and lesser trees provided a cooling shade, Gore forced his way through everything but the thickest bush. The case grew heavier with every step, and he had not gone far before he sat down to rest. The only sounds were the buzzing of insects, the harsh cry of a bird, and a sudden rustling as something ran through the tall grasses to his right.

He would have been surprised that bushes grew so thickly in the shadows of the tall and crowding trees if the inspector had not told him that these bushes were mutations made for these forests, and they thrived on lack of sunlight.

Where he sat was cool and dark, and he could see the bright shafts of sunlight here and there, thrusting down between openings in the forest ceiling. The earth was cool and moist, and the grasses and bushes were green. Once, he understood, this area would have been dusty and the vegetation brown at this time of year. But planetary weather control brought a light rain every other day to this part of California. The land was green throughout the year.

After an estimated ten minutes (his watch had been taken at the border), he got up. He shouldered his pack and started to push on. He broke through the branches of a bush into a clearing and started across it until something buzzed by his ear. He thought it was an insect until he heard a thunking noise coming from a pine about forty feet ahead of him.

He stopped. An arrow was sticking out of the tree.

G ORE'S FIRST THOUGHT WHEN HE SAW THE ARROW AND HEARD running feet crashing through the brush from every direction was that Federal agents had caught up with him. He would have made to run but for the fact that he didn't want to leave behind the valuable wine and get Sir Bobaunce mad at him right at the beginning of his servanthood, possibly nipping in the bud any chance of his rising through Scadia's stratified society.

Of course Federal agents were highly unlikely to come looking for him here. They would respect Scadia's boundaries as they did any such alternative community. And they certainly wouldn't be shooting arrows.

But by the time Gore realized how stupid his thought was, he was surrounded.

It stood to reason that a society recreating lords and ladies, knights and chivalry, and happy peasants in their idyllic fields would also recreate forest-dwelling outlaws. They were even wearing Lincoln green. He wondered if any ballads had been written about them.

"Surrender, knave, or be run through!" a disembodied voice bellowed from the woods, soon to be attached to a man striding into Gore's vision He was tall and lanky with dark curly hair topped by a green floppy hat hung rakishly to one side like the old-fashioned fedoras recently back in style. His face bore a mustache that curled at the end, and a goatee hung from his chin. Like his men, he wore green, only his garb added a gold sash with an elongated lion stretching out its front right paw, claws extended.

"Are you the Green Baron?" Gore asked.

The man slapped his hands to his hips and tilted back with laughter, the mirror image of an old movie Gore once saw starring the 20th century entertainer Errol Flynn.

"Who else should I be, knave?" the Green Baron answered. "Robert o' Hardtooth, if it pleases thee, or if it does not. These woods belong to me and my merry band of brothers. Everything in them belongs to us. Therefore, thou belong to us."

"Sir Bobaunce might have something to say about that," Gore told him.

"Hah! Then let Sir Wastrel of the Stubby Tower come and tell me himself. Though he'll need find me first!"

Gore's hands were tied and he was led even deeper into the woods. Another outlaw picked up the wicker basket, grinning approvingly at its contents, and followed at his master's heels.

At a place where Gore was certain the brush could not grow any thicker and the dim light could scarcely get any dimmer, the Green Baron called a halt. He immediately went for the 2069 bottle and tossed back a long swig. He dried his mouth with his arm theatrically, held up the bottle to the cheers of his men, then commanded them to have at the wine.

Gore caught himself shaking with anger and forced himself to calm down when he felt the narrow-eyed looks two of his captors, one on each side, gave him. Their short swords pointing in his direction looked not quite dull enough to be playthings. Gore wondered where Scadia's strange customs ended and reality began. If he tried to escape, would they actually kill him? Were they role-playing like everyone else here, or were they outlaws in fact as well as name, consigned—condemned?—to these woods because they wouldn't abide by Scadia's rules?

As the outlaws, including his two closest captors, quaffed more and more of the wine, Gore decided there was little point in remaining standing. He sat against the oak where they had left him and watched carefully. The thought of asking anything of the Green Baron, especially about the outlaws' true station in Scadia, was ludicrous. Even if Gore wanted to talk to him, the Baron would just continue playing his role, and might decide Gore was uppity enough that his life should be made extra miserable. He suspected he would get the same reaction from the other outlaws as well.

Amid the greens upon greens Gore noticed a flicker of color out of place. Someone in a far corner of the camp was trying to catch his eye. Not hard, because this man wore a bright blue velvet doublet with equally blue hose and light shoes resembling slippers, not a thing Gore would have preferred for tromping in the woods. Covering his mop of straight brown hair was a thin blue hat drooping behind him like a ponytail. He withdrew a lute from his back and strolled to the center of the camp.

So even the scalawags of the Greenwood had their Alan a' Dale, answering Gore's question to himself about ballads. With a single glance back at Gore, the bard turned his back, facing the outlaw band, and strummed.

The songs were not about the outlaws themselves, but slow, sad tunes about wicked kings forcing innocent men out of their homes, brave men being sent to war and never seeing their wives and sweethearts again, and all manner of other kinds of cruelties the strong could inflict upon the weak.

Gore forced himself not to snicker. None of the outlaws seemed to recognize the irony of such songs in a place where nothing like what they described ever happened, could ever happen. Perhaps they were so deep into their roles they truly believed themselves victims of upper-class atrocities, forced to live like animals among the redwoods and mutant bushes. If nothing else, the music almost exponentially increased their drinking.

They drank so much, in fact, their green-garbed bodies melted languidly into the ground, occasionally releasing great and sundry belches. The two swords previously tipped at Gore acted as if they themselves were tipsy, and sank away. The music changed; the bard was heading toward him, still playing but with only one hand. The other held a slightly rusted but unnecessarily large dagger.

The bard's eyes were intensely blue as he stared at Gore for an instant, then he hacked apart the ropes binding Gore's hands, all while still playing. "My performance here has verily reached its end, sir, and my final bow awaits. Does thou care to accompany me to my next performance?"

What Gore didn't care for was the florid language, even if the bard meant escape. Gore accompanied the bard without a sound of his own, or so he hoped, though he risked jinxing their luck by sliding a quick glance at Robert o' Hardtooth.

One of the leader's eyes was open.

At once Robert o' Hardtooth was on his feet and lunging at Gore with a wicked grin that Gore fancied, in some calm if melodramatic section of his mind, gleamed more than the sword traveling a sure path toward Gore's sternum. Fortunately the rest of Gore's mind had shut down in obsequious deference to his reflexes. He sidestepped the attack easily and one other step brought him behind the Green Baron as if they were engaged in an odd waltz.

The Baron came about for another thrust but whirled where he should have pivoted, allowing Gore to use the Baron's own momentum against him as Gore wrapped one arm around his neck and plunged the Baron's skull into a mighty and unyielding oak.

"Thou should not be late to your next performance," Gore said to the minstrel, his voice steady but the linguistic jumble betraying how shaken he felt. "But I must needs keep an appointment at the Black Tor."

"'Tis as fine a place as any in the Barony," the bard said. They ran. Now and again the blue-wrapped minstrel flashed Gore a look that was all at once admiring and something else. The something else made him edgy.

"Does thou have something to ask me?" Gore asked, an unnamed fear creeping into his craw.

"Nay, good sir, only that thou confirmed my foremost thought that thou were the man to assist and vouchsafe my escape," the bard told him. "For in sooth I was the captive of those scamps for many days, waylaid for their entertainment. I knew such stuff as brave escapes are born of is not found within me alone. Jack o' Japes is my name, friend, and I remain thy servant."

"Will Son of Gore." He instantly regretted revealing the information, though he wasn't certain why.

"I should not care overmuch to make of thou an enemy."

Gore looked deep into the woods—were they heading in the right direction? He wasn't sure. But why would he think the bard might mislead him?

The woods parted as if answering his fears and within moments the Black Tor appeared regally if not loftily above them, a dark, arched sentinel that, if it would mock the gaudy party below it, kept its own counsel.

Sir Bobaunce, still waiting, was looking mightily wroth. He was accompanied by the lustrous Lady Melisounde, who looked sorely befuddled. Alain was nearby with numerous kicks buried within his smug smile. The rest of the hunting party, lords and ladies alike, were as ill-tempered as a drought, not likely far off the mark with the wine pilfered.

"Where have you been, knave?" Sir Bobaunce shouted. "Where have you been at?" he shouted louder, perhaps testing to see if he could shake the Black Tor. He failed.

He failed also to shake Jack o' Japes, whose hand spiraled madly down before him as the vanguard of a deep bow. "My Lord Bobaunce, my eyes feast upon thou with great relief and joy! These past wretched days was I the prisoner of the Green Baron, at the mercy of his rogues' whims. Forced was I to play tunes of most shoddy construction, of tin-eared composition, which would set my lord's melodious heart to vexed palpitating. Verily had I all but given up hope of escape when they likewise brought into their camp good Will Son of Gore, and together did we break free of our savage shackles. But alas, my lord, the wine did not survive the captivity."

"The wine?" Now Sir Bobaunce was indeed wroth, his face such a shade of crimson that Gore wondered with passing fascination if this so-called knight might suffer a stroke, or at least burst his nose. "The Green Baron did abscond with my best vintages!"

Gore forced himself to bow, though he couldn't manage to keep his eyes off the Lady Melisounde. "All he says is true, my good lord."

"To horse!" the swaggering lord shouted, and at once the men were in their saddles, with the master of the hunt blowing a few more peels of his horn that Gore assumed were meant to turn the Green Baron into a fox.

"To horse with you, knave," Bobaunce said to Gore, "and lead us to the scoundrels!"

A servant brought Gore a horse, which he mounted with no small bit of trepidation. Fortunately this animal was a far gentler beast than the one he attempted to ride out of the village, though he knew it would be useless in the woods. He tried to point this out.

"Odsbodkins!" Sir Bobaunce bellowed, which Gore vaguely remembered was some bizarre medieval curse. "If you be a cowardly scab, a scurrilous mongrel, begone with you! I shall hunt down the Green Baron myself! Drink my wine, will he?"

And with that Sir Bobaunce was away—but not into the woods. He took off at a gentle trot down the road, which might as well have led in the direction opposite of the outlaw camp. The hunting party, then the women in sidesaddle, followed at what must have been a suitably deferential distance.

Jack o' Japes caught Gore's sigh. "Aye, isn't it, though?" the bard said with a nearly invisible smirk. "But why hunt outlaws for certes when thou may prolong the merriment with a swell long chase? Better still when the quarry leads thee straight along the highway to the Wicked Duke."

"Aren't they all?" Gore grumbled.

"This be the Wicked Duke of the Castle Dolorous, friend Will, and both, I say in sooth, have earned their monikers." He spurred his horse. "Coming? Thou should not be late for another appointment. His lordship might be most put out."

Gore wanted little more at that moment than to put Sir Bobaunce out a high window. Then he swelled with a longing to put certain things about to M'Lady Melisounde too, and his anger cooled, just a bit. He reminded himself that he could deal with the noxious presence of his knightship when it meant the optical comfort of the lady as recompense.

*T*HE CHASE LED TO THE DOLOROUS CASTLE, AS JACK O' JAPES predicted. It did verily—Gore twisted his lip realizing he was already thinking in Scadia's odd dialect—live up to its moniker. Amid the lush Greenwood in this corner of the Barony of Scadia, the castle was a Brobdingnagian gray monolith interrupting the surrounding color like a policeman breaking up an amorous couple in the park.

Gore studied the dreary stone carbuncle and wondered how far the Scadians would take the notion that they were recreating the Middle Ages as they should have been. Would the Castle Dolorous be all stone and mortar, susceptible to the flaws and inconveniences of its medieval counterparts? Or would it have surreptitiously incorporated 22nd century building materials and advancements?

Probably not, Gore thought. Such could explain why the Dolorous Castle was so dolorous and the Wicked Duke so wicked.

A few none-too-happy-looking guards about the front battlements took notice of the approaching party and blew three blasts of a horn similar to the one Sir Bobaunce had used to gain entry to his own castle. The drawbridge creaked open like a crippled arthritic being roused from sleep and collapsed with a thud that Gore was surprised didn't crack it apart.

A guard strolled halfway across the drawbridge, bowed sharply but shallowly, then announced, "My lord and master, Duke Marrok of the Castle Dolorous, bids ye enter and partake of his hospitality and his leisure." Another curt bow, and the guard returned to his station while stablehands scurried about to relieve the party of their horses.

"My good Sir Bobaunce!" Marrok bellowed upon their entering what Gore presumed was the Feasting Hall: on the far end was a stone fireplace of the same bleak gray as the rest of the castle, its hearth large enough to accommodate several guests should they want to try it.

From hearth to door stretched an oaken table and equally long benches, with the requisite scruffy hounds chewing on well-shredded bones. The man Gore assumed was the Wicked Duke was singing at the top of his lungs, and Gore suddenly realized that was why there was nothing delicate in the castle—it would shatter under Duke Marrok's foghorn of a voice.

For certes he shattered the otherwise lovely voices of the three women around him. They were dressed alike in bright flowing red, a veritable riot of color compared to the rest of the place, with conical hats draping silk behind them. The Duke notwithstanding, they were attempting to sing a song repeating the word *Gaudete* in the chorus.

At last the Wicked Duke halted his music-butchering and asked, "Are thou hungry, Bobaunce? I am starving on my feet and shall be presented with beef anon. I have eaten naught for at least two hours!" His laughter closely resembled his singing.

As he left behind the singing ladies Gore noticed that his hands slid deftly across the folds of two of their backsides. Their faces remained as stony as the walls and they barely missed a note; obviously they were accustomed to such treatment.

He invited Sir Bobaunce and Lady Melisounde to a seat by the head of the table, then plunked his lean posterior on the bench beside m'lady. He swept her hand to his lips and placed a kiss upon her knuckles that seemed overlong, while never removing his eyes from the lady's. Gore felt a flash of jealousy, though he could hardly blame the Duke. It also reinforced his idea that becoming a Scadian peasant was a bad idea. A sodbuster would hardly have the chance to kiss the lady's hand, much less anything else upon her person.

Jealousy flared again when Duke Marrok placed a hand on her arm, then her shoulder, then not-so-discreetly slid his arm around her and spoke softly and closely as a lover would, which Gore suspected Marrok wished to be, justifiably. Sir Bobaunce was beet-faced but kept his chatter to polite small talk. So the Wicked Duke outranked his Booze-ship, then.

Duke Marrok only released his grip on the blushing lady when the beef emerged, carried forth on a great platter by four men as if the whole cow was being served in a single sitting. There was a tug on Gore's sleeve; Jack o' Japes was gesturing that they were to dine in another room, the one reserved for servants, adding they would get their share of oxflesh only after the nobles had been properly served—and just as properly given second and third helpings.

"I hear Duke Marrok isn't such a bad sort," the bard said with confiding quiet. "From a certain point of view. The ladies may possess a harsher view, but then, I have also heard not all of them reject his mouth-dribbling advances. Either way, all agree he is much of an improvement upon the last Wicked Duke."

"The last Wicked Duke? I don't get—I take not your meaning, minstrel."

"The previous denizen of the Castle Dolorous," Jack o' Japes explained. "Apparently he made merry by attacking other castles on a right regular year-round schedule. The only one he did naught to anger was the Green Baron, as he ne'er caught the Baron either."

Once again Gore wondered where reality ended and play began. He was starting to believe the Green Baron and the Wicked Duke were institutions, with certain subtle rules opponents obeyed. He didn't understand them yet but planned to continue watching carefully. For certes no one in Scadia would simply voice them outright.

Jack motioned to Gore with a single finger and he whispered, "'Tis hardly unknown for men to seek the conquest of women—has it not been so in every age? And women themselves can be quite cunning and make themselves seem conquered when they're a-doing the conquering, in sooth. But my lord Wicked Duke boasts about his feminine surrenders, which is forbidden. 'Tis rumored he is also not above abducting a fair damsel from time to time. But none will come forward with proof, damsels or otherwise, so naught is spoken about it."

The lack of proof wasn't the only reason nothing was said, Gore suspected. Kidnapping was a Federal crime. If the authorities got wind of it they would step in and arrest him. Scadia's illusions would be broken.

Gore shook his head wordlessly. The Wicked Duke sounded like nothing more than a college fraternity brother. He wondered if any of Scadia's mascots had turned up stolen, or its maidens' panties raided.

"There is still more," Jack pressed. "He asks for ransoms which are exceeding high according to the Code, and he keeps his prisoners—knights he has defeated in combat, albeit fair combat—locked up until ransom is paid. Most unchivalrous." Jack punctuated his declaration with a disapproving scowl. "And yet, as I ken, still better than the erstwhile duke."

Something clicked in Gore's mind. While Scadia had been in existence for some years now—decades, long enough for many of its residents to have been born and spent their whole lives here—Gore obviously could not have been the only traveler to seek shelter in its walls. They didn't advertise themselves; in fact, the Scadians went out of their way to be as isolated as possible. But as Gore proved, they still did allow immigrants inside their walls, no questions asked.

The way Jack o' Japes talked, he didn't seem to be a native. Gore found himself wondering who the bard had been before he vacated the Outside. Perhaps he had not even been in Scadia much longer than Gore himself.

As if reading his thoughts and wanting to contradict them, Jack said, "From whereabouts come thou, good friend Will? I ne'er saw thy face ere our cunning escape from the outlaw peril."

"I have naught to distinguish me," he said. He felt silly mangling the language, but supposed it was much like the embarrassment of your first trip to a nude beach. Why be self-conscious when everyone else was similarly bare? Or perhaps a more appropriate metaphor would be ignoring one's own smell when no one else had taken a bath. Either way, he didn't want to sound fresh from the Outside.

"For certes, all have something I use to discern them," Jack told him.

"'Tis a matter of survival. I learn faces, I do, and then what sorts of songs suit and please those faces best."

"I like not any songs about outlaws," Gore said.

The minstrel guffawed and clapped Gore on the shoulder. As if on cue the beef emerged, now cut into strips from the original beast but no less thick or juicy for all that. It was quite tasty, especially when washed down with cold, sweet mead, and Jack o' Japes spoke no more about Gore himself. But Gore was still left unsettled, and vowed he would be more careful about what information he revealed—perhaps how much he even spoke in general—to the bard.

Two flagons of mead later, he wasn't so certain what he was afraid of. Jack didn't even have the nerve to escape the outlaws, after all. After his third and final flagon, Gore wasn't so certain why he would be afeared of anyone or anything at all in Scadia.

Gore may have been pleased to quaff a fourth flagon—as the Wicked Duke's servants explained, quaffing was not discouraged as long as one could still work, and drank only what was offered rather than what the nobles wanted for themselves—except he was interrupted by a thunderous roar from the Great Hall. The servants' dining room door swung open and Sir Bobaunce himself filled the space, and he threw his hand into the air in a gesture worthy of an overbearing thespian.

"Out, exeunt, all of ye, make haste! Duke Marrok's men have spotted a dragon scarcely one hundred yards from the Castle Dolorous, prowling the woods and beating its great wings to launch an attack against the duke's livestock and damosels, without doubt!" He glared at Gore, who was suddenly grateful he still had feeling in his legs after so much honey-booze. "My mount, knave, if you wish to redeem yourself in my eyes!"

Probably not so easy in such bloodshot eyes, Gore mused, but he made as much haste as the sloshing in his stomach would allow. Inside of five minutes Sir Bobaunce's and the Wicked Duke's squires had armored them up; one minute later the knights were both on their steeds, swords drawn and their calls of "Halloo!" echoing through the forest. Gore searched the trees for sight of the dragon—or whatever it was that passed for a dragon in Scadia.

The knights rode ahead, leaving Gore to follow in their dust. As he coughed, his brain reviewed what little he knew of genetic manipulation. Perhaps their "dragon" was an overblown iguana, or a gila monster with delusions of grandeur, or a crocodile with a Napoleon complex.

At any rate, he was sure the fools bobbing ahead of him would make short work of the fearsome beast, and then return to the castle for more beef and wine and prodding Jack o' Japes to write a song about their adventure.

Then Gore rounded the corner where the fight ensued.

The dragon was—a dragon.

It was forty feet long from emerald bow to stern, boasting occipital ridges across its head, bone-plated spikes running down its elongated neck through its equally elongated tail, and a spiked bone club at tail's tip. Furthermore it had wings half as long as its body. They were so thin as to be translucent but whipped up a mighty wind. If Gore was much closer he would have been knocked off his feet by the wormgale. Its eyes were gold and serpentine, and its fangs as long as Gore's forearm.

Gore watched in tipsy befuddlement as Sir Bobaunce galloped at the creature, sword aloft, shouting, "Yoikes! Have at you, pet of Cain!"

Befuddlement turned, ironically, into a numb chill when the dragon blasted Sir Bobaunce off his horse with a stream of fire and sent the rest of the party flying.

Then the dragon turned his golden gaze slowly, inexorably, on Gore.

Gore found himself wishing he were still a prisoner of the Green Baron.

*G*ORE RAN NOT QUITE TO SIR BOBAUNCE'S SIDE, AS DOING SO would quickly close his distance from the dragon. But he found an oblique point where he could get a better view of the damage.

Only Sir Bobaunce's red-barred triple beer-stein shield had saved him from being toasted in his armor. He had small burns here and there, enough to keep the knight awake at night less pleasantly than the Lady Melisounde, but nothing life-threatening. His horse was less fortunate.

All of these thoughts ran through Gore's head in the seconds before the dragon drew a bead on them again. Gore reached for his dagger before remembering it was left back at the castle.

He made to beat a hasty retreat but the dragon was surprisingly fast; he curved around the knights like quicksilver on rising metal and then his gold eyes were perched just feet away from Gore.

Gore froze. Even if he'd had a sword he had no idea how to use one without hurting himself. Whatever the dragon wanted to do with him, it could.

The dragon did nothing.

Gore heard a squeak not far enough behind him. M'lady Melisounde watched him with rapt horror. Hands leaped to her mouth as soon as the dragon decided she was worth its attention, too. But still it did nothing.

Until Sir Palamides led the charge with a flashing scimitar. Then the dragon let out a bone-shattering roar and leaped only an instant behind the flood of fire erupting from its mouth. At that moment Gore noticed it catch sight of a young servant woman holding the hand of a small girl, no more than five, both of whom must have been deaf to walk this far down the road without hearing the raucous worm. Once more the dragon ignored them in favor of the armed men.

Spurred on by the flash of a wretched idea, Gore made for Sir Bobaunce and placed himself between the knight and the dragon. Again, not out of any chivalrous impulses on Gore's part, but because Gore didn't want the dragon to see him slip the sword into his belt behind his back.

He dared a look at the Lady Melisounde to swell his courage and perhaps stimulate the production of extra testosterone, the way males were encouraged to do vaunted and stupid feats throughout the ages. Making certain his hands were empty, Gore lunged at the dragon.

This move served to annoy the beast momentarily, but it merely flapped its wings, nearly sending Gore off his feet, before returning its attention to the knights, who still were having poor fortune at killing it. His suspicions confirmed, Gore pulled free his blade the instant the dragon looked away and then buried the weapon up to the hilt squarely in the center of the soft, unprotected neck.

The dragon slammed Gore away with its bony head.

Its serpentine eyes focused on this pale-fleshed source of its pain and prepared for Gore a cathartic blast of fire. But a gurgle erupted in place of flames; instead of a bellow, the dragon squeaked. Its eyes widened with pained surprise, and then a broadsword through its temple robbed the gold from its gaze forever. It toppled to the ground with barely a puff of dirt.

"I have slaughtered the scourge!" the Wicked Duke shouted, his gauntleted fists raised in triumph.

Gore ignored him, more interested in getting a close-up look at the thing that so nearly caused his demise. Blood flowed freely, but it was blood that smoked. While he may have simply attributed this to steam otherwise, or perhaps the kinds of hot innards that might give rise to fire-breathing, Gore also saw broken pieces of metal in the dark fluid, as well as unmistakable wires and computer chips. He placed his hand on the dragon's skin. It was cool and slick as a reptile's should be.

So it was a robot. Gore, who had tinkered with robots from childhood and made them the foundation of what became his fortune before he went on the lam, stared at the machine with professional interest.

It was a very clever machine with electronics and protoplasm for its insides, and real skin, possibly even bone, for its body. A robot programmed—as Gore guessed correctly, so much the better for him—to leave be women and children and unarmed men, as it thought Gore was. It would, however, react with an attack to certain stimuli: anyone bearing arms.

"So the dragon has its own place here," Gore thought out loud. "All positions—the Wicked Duke, the Green Baron, and the Menacing Dragon. And if humans can be replaced, perhaps we'll see another dragon savaging the countryside sooner or later . . . "

"Clamp thy insolent mouth, villein!" the Wicked Duke shouted. "Your maundering ramblings set my gizzard on edge!"

Gore clamped down his reply. Obviously the Scadians wanted no external commentary on their schizophrenic society.

Yet the next voice Gore heard was the angelic melody of Lady Melisounde. "I beg pardon, M'lord, but it was good Will Son of Gore who dealt the deathblow. Am I mistaken, husband?"

Sir Bobaunce managed to regain his feet, and tugged his drooping moustache. "M'lady's observation is clear and pure," he said. "'Twas my own stableboy what did the deed."

Gore suspected Sir Bobaunce would have said so even if it weren't true. It was simply a way to strike back at the Wicked Duke's advances on Lady Melisounde.

No matter. M'lady's voice was still ringing in his ear like a gold hand-bell. He allowed himself to hope that the lady had stood up for him for himself, not as her own method of payback.

"So thou say," the Wicked Duke answered, eyes narrowed. "But now thou must needs elevate yon stableboy to knighthood. If thou hold to thy claim, Lord of High Tower, I should much revel in watching thou teach this lout the proper courtesies."

Sir Bobaunce sniffed. "Care for a wager, my lord Duke?"

Duke Marrok grinned. "Mayhaps a single gold crown?"

Gore heard little more of the terms of their bet. For another idea had flashed into his mind: even the so-called lowest born peasant could work his way up to king, with enough ambition, patience, and a sufficiently stiff buttocks to resist boots. Gore had just taken the first step for advancement, bringing him one step closer to luring the Lady Melisounde—legitimately, within Scadia's Code—to his bedchamber.

At last Sir Bobaunce stood before Gore and surveyed him with a belittling scowl. "A knight you must be, knave, therefore a knight you shall be. You shall become my new squire, I wit, and prepare thyself for a myriad magnificent blows. For I shall have you trained and ready to compete under my banner at the tourney in Camelot a fortnight hence." The scowl deepened. "What say you, knave?"

Gore forced himself to utter, "Thankee, sire." From the corner of his eye he caught Lady Melisounde's bright grin. He also caught an all-too-pleased look from Alain the bootspeaker.

The Wicked Duke let forth a chuckle Gore would have called sinister had it been in a movie. "Thou shall sore regret this, Sir Bobaunce, mark me. Regret indeed." He waved toward the dead horse. "Attend to thy mess!"

Then he mounted his horse, spun around with a flourish, and beat a narrow path back to Castle Dolorous.

*O*NE GOOD THING ABOUT BEING SIR BOBAUNCE'S SQUIRE WAS that it meant moving into the Castle of the High Tower. This included a new mattress for Gore filled with feathers rather than straw, even if he did arrive every night bruised and battered.

For all of his master's paunch, for all of his drinking and florid cheeks and inflated nose, the knight knew his business when it came to combat. The dragonfire must have been a lucky hit, for Gore—no weakling, and who knew empirically that he could kill a man—had yet to score any hit at all.

It stood to reason. Sir Bobaunce had probably given himself over to knighthood and training for as long as he had been in Scadia, which meant he likely had years of a head start on Gore.

Gore was strong, but most of his fighting skills emerged only when his life was threatened or he flew into a murderous rage—once literally. Sir Bobaunce made certain his new squire was soundly banged and smacked during his hours-a-day high-pressure streamlined training, but Gore never had the sense that Sir Bobaunce would put him in mortal danger. At the very least, he wanted Gore to show up the Wicked Duke's champion at the swiftly approaching Camelot Tourney.

"You are ignorant, knave," Sir Bobaunce said early on, still clinging to the hated class usages until Gore proved himself. "But you show a shard of a glimpse of promise. And you have no better master in all the barony!"

So Gore practiced sunup to sundown day after grueling day.

Compared to these workouts, his Muscle Beach series of homemade training robots were ninety-pound weaklings waiting for Sir Bobaunce to kick sand in their faces.

He would have to reassess his chances if Sir Bobaunce demanded single combat to restore his besmirched honor should—when—Gore made his move on his master's lady. But he became more of a match for the knight with every sunset. He also reflected that his added strength, reflexes, and aim would be put to excellent use upon a successful seduction.

One thing did weigh sore upon his mind, though: the constant presence and frequent questioning—all but interrogations, Gore thought—of the ubiquitous minstrel Jack o' Japes. He had also spied Friend Jack engaging in several conversations with the right ignoble Alain.

At last, one evening while Gore was shadow-fencing in the castle courtyard and ignoring the gaze of Jack o' Japes on his back while the bard idly strummed a lute, his suspicions bloomed fully formed and momentarily froze him both in shock and recognition.

Jack o' Japes was, Gore believed, a Federal agent.

No doubt in Scadia to determine whether or not he would be able to haul Gore back Outside on charges of murder.

Only a month—a lifetime!—past, Gore was an incredibly successful businessman whose face nobody knew but whose Silent Running series of robots everybody wanted. Because his robots didn't just do household chores—they were "fidos" who went running for information on the computer nets, who could enact and negotiate certain delicate transactions, who could sniff out information that was otherwise locked . . .

All anonymously.

Just as Gore was anonymous, a handsome young face among California's beautiful and rich. Nearly everyone liked him though very few knew why he was invited to so many parties. They assumed he was simply popular, or a big contributor to political campaigns, or anything else but the truth.

On his final day of freedom and using the name he was born with twenty-three years before, Jason Caerwyn, he was enjoying the company of two beautiful and rich ladies during the incumbent governor's post-

post-post inaugural soiree on the dance floor of the official 74th floor Sacramento condominium.

He rarely imbibed alcohol, though his constitution could handle quite a bit. Not so the constitution of one Luis Chang O'Smith, state senator from El Centro. O'Smith was known primarily for grafting pounds of flesh from his taxpayers onto his own sizeable girth. He was known secondarily for being a pugnacious fight-starter after a few gin-and-sangrias neat, and decided he wanted a piece of the action of two sunburned platinum blondes who, at that particular moment, were making pleasant small talk with Gore about his robots' brands of cold fusion "nuggets" for power supplies and Gore's own personal power requirements.

Gore's next memories contained a few shared arrogant words and O'Smith physically manifesting his memories of youthful boxing. Gore rarely challenged anyone but never refused a challenge.

There were screams from the ladies, a full-on frontal assault from the senator, who had managed to maneuver Gore between himself and the railing, and a red haze dripping into Gore's eyes.

All of those present testified that Gore flinging the senator away, and consequently over the 74th floor balcony railing, was justifiable homicide. But the judge decided the defendant reacted too swiftly.

By Gore's time murderers were no longer incarcerated or executed. They were not, however, dealt with lightly. Gore's fate would be getting packed off to a maximum security mental hospital for drug therapy combined with the cutting edge of 22nd century psychotherapy, including computers constantly recording his brain patterns, his thoughts and dreams, his most fleeting idea burned into his permanent record and available to every hospital, policeman, reporter, government agent, and anyone else with a credit chip and a desire to run a background check. For the rest of his life he would tool about with an ID chip implanted in his brain.

In addition, good doctors were at a premium. The process could take years before a judge decided him "cured", deemed safe to return to society, and released. They would also little care that Gore suffered a neurosis about being locked up or even just in too-close quarters.

He swiftly decided he was not in favor of such treatment.

He had heard of Scadia but never given it much thought before. They went to great lengths to preserve their secrecy; Gore could appreciate this, doing the same himself. All he knew was that it was an alternative community set out in what most people—those content to remain in their tiny apartments in a megalopolis—considered to be an unsettled and unsettling wilderness. But those who wanted to leave the cities were welcome to do so. Those proving they could build a self-sufficient alternative community to help relieve the environmental devastation of the first half of the 21st century were given space in the national parks to do so.

The government had parceled off a large section of northern California to the Scadians forty years before and, per the Quadripartisan Alternative Communities Act of 2045 that helped bring about the Economy of Abundance the second half of the 21st century enjoyed, agreed not to interfere in their affairs except in the direst emergency.

Perhaps the self-defense killing of an admittedly unpleasant state senator would not be considered dire. But covering his bets, Gore sent out word through his Silent Running fidos to each and every one of his clients that should a Pete—a P.T., Psychoneurotic Therapist—apprehend Gore, he would broker a deal with the government by giving them all of his robot-cloak tech . . . along with his client list, which included Federal officials, kept on a nanobit he injected into a particularly hard-to-reach area of pelvic bone.

In other words, it would be in the best interest of all involved if Gore was never found.

He rebelled at the idea of hiding in Scadia at first. He made his fortune by the highest of high-tech; his villa near the New Pacific Coast Highway was filled with every conceivable luxury—female companionship included—and he possessed little desire to spend the rest of his life roughing it. But after fleeing from the authorities the idea of finding Scadia and hiding within it developed into an obsession.

He dispatched Silent Running fidos to study as much Medieval history as he could. But he only snagged bits and pieces, little more than trivia—

and a place to buy himself garb for the gates—before his instincts told him to wipe their caches and get running. And he always suffered when he ignored his instincts.

Now he was beginning to believe, as Milton's Devil did, 'twas better to reign in Hell than serve in Heaven. If Jack o' Japes verily was a Federal agent, he would have to be watched closely, and dealt with if necessary.

At the end of the ninth day of sparring, Sir Bobaunce responded to Gore's short bow by saying, "Prepare your traveling gear, knave. In the morn we ride for Camelot."

"Is not the tourney still several days off, sire?" Gore asked. He was not fully considered a knight yet, but Sir Bobaunce had granted Gore the privilege of speaking not just when spoken to or in case of emergency. Though Gore was to have a care if the subject dealt with aught but weapons or other combat-related topics.

"Knave, once more you prove your ignorance of our ways here. There will be a fair number of days of feasting, fighting, and fussing ere the tourney, of which even you may avail yourself. Only a boor would arrive in Camelot at the appointed hour."

Gore stood amid the courtyard, considering his possibilities, long after his beefy master returned to the castle to avail himself of another dinner and, no doubt, Lady Melisounde's bountiful cornucopia. A veritable buffet, she was.

The feastings and festivities should provide many chances in which to win her heart a piece at a time—or at least her favor.

He also did not miss Jack o' Japes' absence from his normal spot at the edge of the courtyard. No doubt the malignant minstrel would be present as well, singing for his supper. Gore would keep as sharp an eye on him as he did the behavioral and self-determination algorithms of the first robots that built the foundation of his own erstwhile kingdom.

*G*ALLOPING ACROSS HIGH TOWER'S DRAWBRIDGE TO JOIN THE rest of the household preparing for the excursion to Camelot, Gore felt as if he were joining in a medieval convoy. Which, in effect, he was.

Nearly every man, woman, and in some cases child from the castle and its immediate environs had donned garb competing for who could out-bright everyone else. There were standard bearers carrying the same red-barred and beer-steined design on the pennants Sir Bobaunce had on his shield. (Fortunately he had more than one shield, as the other was still being scourged of the signs of dragonfire.)

So many people rode and walked behind Gore, who took his place near the front, he imagined himself at the head of the King's Progress itself. For a moment he placed himself in the boots of the king of Scadia, then duke for life. The fancy left a warm and filling taste in his mouth.

Gore knew Scadia was enormous, maybe even hundreds of square miles and made artificially larger by its convoluted road system. But he hadn't thought to ask how long the trip to Camelot would be. At the end of the first day's travel, a saddle-sore Gore rode up to Sir Bobaunce and the Lady Melisounde, who rode under a great red-and-gold shade held up by young servants on either side of them, "Sire, prithee, how far is it to Camelot?"

"Another two days hence," the knight replied with the satisfaction of one covered by shade and sipping cool booze constantly refreshed.

But Gore surprised himself: the saddle sores began to fade (or were forgotten in the aches and pains of each evening sparring) and he found himself greatly enjoying the languid pace now that he was no longer a mere stableboy. He too earned cool drinks, at least now and again. As well as the warming glances of the occasional bright-eyed nubile serving girl.

They skirted the edge of the dark and thick Perilous Woods, from which odd sounds and the occasional cry escaped. But Gore paid little heed to them.

There were also taverns placed along the road every few miles, and Sir Bobaunce was quite particular about where he stayed. Gore had no doubt he chose the best, and he was now able to get his own room as another benefit of his station. He ate well on Sir Bobaunce's tab, and was able to acquire a taste for Scadia's variety of beverages as long as he did not quaff overmuch—whatever that meant.

Each night brought more drinks and fresh linens from one of his master's maids. Each night the maid stayed with Gore, ministering to him of her substance, longer than may have been proper but well within Scadia's unwritten Code. At the Chanticleer and every other stop Gore was the cock-o'-the-walk. Even the lowliest classes of Scadia's women could not be coerced, forced, or threatened; but neither were they forbidden to set their caps on whomever they may.

So different from Gore's frenetic lifestyle Outside. There he jaunted from party to party, meeting to meeting, office to office, politician to politician, woman to woman. Life in this rustic place took on entirely new depths of color when Gore was forced to slow down.

He realized he was coming perilously close to being a happy man. He muttered a not-quite-insincere thankee to the macho delusions of one Senator Luis Chang O'Smith, late of El Centro, California.

They reached Camelot at the onset of dusk of the third day. The sun was red and gold, similar to but richer than Sir Bobaunce's shades. The land and the city reflected those lavish and generous hues even more deeply, as if both believed themselves eternal and challenged the sky in their pride.

And here rose what Gore knew must be Scadia's model city: Camelot, comprised mainly of towers and steeples and flags and stunningly colored clothes glowing in the falling twilight.

Gore had thought the village clean, but here it seemed even the streets conspired to keep their material to themselves and in place. Tiled roofs shined, there was nary a mound of manure to be seen in the streets. The chimney smoke was neither overpowering nor too pale to be worth considering. The children's faces were perfectly scrubbed and, Gore couldn't help but think, no doubt the small stubborn spots behind their small ears were too.

The castle rose clifflike from a sharp but not forbidding rise above the city, all uncrumbling glory, beneficent power, firm but fair vision-impaired justice. Gore wondered briefly if the king and queen had happened to make laws regarding Camelot's temperature and precipitation as well.

As Gore guessed and hoped, the Knight's Progress wound an unhurried serpentine path to the castle, where it would lodge itself through the duration of the tourney and perhaps some rambunctious days afterward. Camelot Castle towered over its other Scadian counterparts like a leviathan lording over a backyard pond. Gore had no doubt that the Progress of every duke, knight, and whatever other noble class Scadia might boast could all take quarters here with plenty of elbow room to spare.

Sir Bobaunce misinterpreted the gleam in Gore's gaze. "Do not believe for a moment, knave, that you may loaf and lounge about in Camelot as you did the taverns," he warned. "You ken this be permitted in travel, for the road is hard, and eating dust is the lot of every man. But here you are my squire, and you shall behave as such."

Gore fought down his smirk. "I am at thy service, sire. I need only instructions pertaining to thine expectations of me."

The knight grunted. "You may feast, Will Son of Gore, and you shall make pleasantries with the damsels, o' course." Did Melisounde's smile brighten just a bit?

Then the knight continued, "But hereabouts you pay for your leisure. You will accept every challenge, issue challenges of your own, and give a nod to myself and M'lady at the commencement of each engagement. This is not the tourney but you must ne'er slack for all that. Think of these happy days as the first course of a great banquet."

The thought of a banquet brought other delicious desserts to Gore's mind, but for once he squelched them. He suspected a fresh squire would be a primary object of challenge and planned to keep his mind on his sword.

He was proven correct more quickly than he had anticipated.

The challenges were, indeed, waiting for him when they passed through the portcullis and into the castle. No fewer than four other knights had placed their names beside his on a great contest board mounted above the monumental fireplace in the Feasting Hall—a room easily three times the size of his master's and the Wicked Duke's, with a table to match.

The Royal Master-at-Arms, Sir Odoacer von Thuringia, was a small-eyed man possessing a muscle-filled body nearly large enough to rival the castle itself. All muscle and no fat under the plate mail, Gore suspected. From him Gore learned he could take three of the challenges when it pleased him (albeit waiting overlong was suspect). But in respecting tradition and the courtesy of his royal hosts, King Marhaus and Queen Brangwaine, one challenge must be fought tonight.

Being the one challenged, it was Gore's right to choose the first contender. He surveyed the names chalked in next to his. It might seem cowardly to choose the weakest first—if weak any were—but Gore also was reluctant to choose the strongest until he could gauge what he was up against.

'Twas was a moot point. He recognized none of the knights' names; he knew nothing of their reputations, strong or weak—if weak any were. At the conclusion of his thoughtful interlude he simply chose the first name on the list. His decision roused what Gore thought was an inordinate "Hip Hip Huzzah!" until he realized his would be the first skirmish of the pre-Tourney days.

They would, Sir Odoacer informed him, be fighting in the throne room, within certain boundaries the mountain of a man set out. The audience would be the King and Queen of Camelot, as they would attend every bout. The rules were simple: three strikes and you were out. One hit counted as one strike.

Complicating matters, a strike on a limb removed it from the rest of the duel. If your sword arm was hit, you were obliged to transfer your blade to the other hand and hold the "lopped" arm behind your back. If a leg were "shorn off", down you went on that knee.

At length the Royal Master-at-Arms added that were you to step out of the boundary, a bright red bunting laid in a wide square across the center of the throne room floor, it counted against you as a hit.

The royal couple arrived: King Marhaus was a man of long curly blonde hair and short curly beard and bearing a gold band of a crown with gem-encrusted steeples. He was nearly the mirror image of an ancient gold bust of Charlemagne Gore had once seen in a museum in Germany, and he thought the resemblance was probably not coincidence.

Queen Brangwaine was quietly stunning in a more earthy than regal way. Her face was plain skin and eyes like the Pacific Ocean was plain water and salt. She walked with a casual gait the way the wind made a casual rustling in the leaves at the sky-piercing peaks of the redwoods. She wore a simple emerald dress, with sleeves nearly touching to the floor, the way California had turned a simple emerald from its lifelong brown after weather modification brought soft and regular rains.

His opponent stood ready in the audience and was introduced as Duke Ambrose, not Sir Ambrose per the listing on the challenge chart. So not only could a man rise above his rank, a simple squire could fight a duke. And the lack of a noble title on the chart implied that with swords in hand, all men were equals, in the way death was egalitarian.

Duke Ambrose lunged, and Gore would remember little of the fight afterward.

He remembered several arrogant challenges which fell on deaf ears, a few obvious feints, a plethora of lunges more theatrical than cunning. Gore danced a bit but otherwise saved his strength. Here and there he made a feint that by design was even more obvious than the duke's. So when he did make a real thrust it seemed to not only surprise but affront the duke. He whacked Gore's sword away petulantly, and Gore used the momentum to arc the blade around and give Ambrose a sound smack in the side of his helmet.

He hadn't thought the blow so mighty, but the duke went down.

Suspicious, Gore inspected the fallen knight carefully. Then with no further hesitation he tapped the tip of his sword once on the duke's sword arm, then his other.

"Three blows, with both arms removed from combat!" the Royal Master-at-Arms shouted, followed by yet another hearty "Hip Hip Huzzah!" from the audience. Gore hadn't thought his own performance especially praiseworthy, but the royal couple's clapping, he admitted, was too brisk to be simply polite.

E'en better, the ferocious scowl blackening Duke Marrok's visage was matched only by the ferocious pleasure in the Lady Melisounde's grin.

Alain too had a ferocious grin, but of a different sort. "Not bad for thy opening bout, my Lord of the Unclean Shovel," he whispered. He turned his hindquarters to Gore, bowed floridly to the royal couple, and simultaneously offered Gore an equally pungent fart.

"Care for a tourney of our own, odorous codpiece?" Gore replied.

"You have no right to challenge me," Alain said. "Not while we serve under the same master, anyroad. But when I am knighted anon . . . "

Gore wondered if a boot to the rear counted as a strike. And if Alain could fight with his ass removed from the sparring.

Later that night, Gore was seated three spaces away from the Lady Melisounde, but she brushed him with praising whispers whenever she chanced to pass by, which happened more often than Gore ascribed to chance.

At one point she told him, "Thou made progress in thy training far more swiftly than anyone imagined, Goodman Will. Now thou are hight Sir Will One Blow among many of this good company. Will thou fell thy remaining opponents so swiftly?"

She offered her hand, and he kissed it.

Gore answered, "I will lay as many hits as thou desires, M'lady."

Her lips flushed and she twirled a lock of hair. At that moment, Gore felt more powerful than when he controlled a chain of one hundred robots from a single switchboard.

And so went the next two nights, a shining haze of feasting and drinking. And music—some from Jack o' Japes, including lute duets with one Senor Ibanez. For the first time since his arrival in Scadia, Gore heard British accents mingling with German, French, Italian, Scandinavian, and from elsewhere in Europe. Here and there he even caught Arabic and other farther-flung tongues.

There were also more than a handful of passing comments from the Lady Melisounde. Not only did he feel invincible, he apparently was. While it took more than a single blow to the helm to rout his remaining opponents, and verily he did break a sweat with each and take two hits from two of them, he still finished them off one by one without a single misstep outside the bunting.

Each time M'lady watched him with flushed lips, twirled hair, and what Gore could not mistake but was a smoldering stare. At the conclusion of his third challenge she delicately pulled a violet kerchief from her cleavage and offered it to Gore. "My favor, Sir Knight," she told him. "If thou will be my champion, it is thine to return to me at thy desire."

Gore pressed the kerchief against his heart and bowed deeply, not removing his eyes from the lady. So she was in love with him now, he was certain. Nothing would turn him from his path.

Nothing except the Wicked Duke. He chose that otherwise most propitious moment to make his move on Melisounde.

He pulled her against him and leered down her cleavage. "Mayhap there be another for me, M'lady?" he bellowed, his laughter rolling down into her dress. "Nay? Then I must needs locate another article of use?" He thrust his hand through her plunging neckline.

"Enough, varlet!" Sir Bobaunce shouted. "I shall tolerate no more of thy insolence! Have at thee!"

Duke Marrok instantly parried Sir Bobaunce's blow as if he'd expected it, which no doubt he had. Sir Bobaunce was no slouch, as Gore could testify to with the still-swelling purple splotches across his body.

But Duke Marrok fought like a machine. His blade was almost a blur and he showed no signs of tiring. Gore watched Sir Bobaunce's hopes for the kingship fade in his eyes as they weakened.

Marrok's slightest thrusts forced Sir Bobaunce to retreat. The knight tripped over the bunting, and a swinging cut hurled Gore's master's sword into the air. Halfway down another swing by the Wicked Duke opened up Sir Bobaunce's sword arm and the knight's agonized cry filled the throne room.

King Marhaus and Queen Brangwaine both jumped to their feet, but neither made a move to stop the Wicked Duke. Whatever powers they claimed over Scadia did not include interfering with a challenge, not when made plainly over besmirched honor.

So neither they nor anyone else moved when the Wicked Duke lifted his broadsword above Sir Bobaunce's panting chest and thrust downwards.

*F*OR THE FIRST TIME SINCE ENTERING SCADIA, GORE HAD what he may have considered a chivalrous impulse. While still owning little love for Sir Bobaunce, he liked Duke Marrok far less, and was riled at the thought of the Wicked Duke striking down an unarmed injured man. These two feelings resulted in Gore's sword crossing with the Duke's several inches above Sir Bobaunce's chest.

Unfortunately, the Wicked Duke was a far better swordsman than Gore as well.

A few thunderous blows smacked Gore's sword until Gore felt as if his arm was about to shake out of its socket. The next blow smashed the blade out of Gore's hand and sliced open the back of his hand in the process. Next a lightning kick to Gore's chest sent him flying backwards.

The familiar red haze filled Gore's vision and he did nothing to stop it. But still the Wicked Duke was faster—the next blow was the flat of the blade against the back of Gore's skull, sending him down to the floor with both world and brain spinning.

He heard more clanging swords and another cry of pain from the next loser, not the Duke. By the time Gore was finally able to rally himself enough to sit up without the world yanking itself away from his vision, the Wicked Duke was shouting, "I challenge every knave in this room!" He pointed his sword at King Marhaus. "Aye, even you, my liege!"

An angry cry arose; Gore wondered if it was born from the challenge or the improper use of Scadian linguistics.

Sir Bobaunce was carried to his room after his wounds were tended. Likewise, Gore's stinging hand was given a dark salve that made it sting even more, then bandaged. All night long the ceiling seemed to press down on his chest like a stone crushing a confession of witchcraft out of him.

If there was one thing able to remove women from Gore's mind entirely, it was humiliation. Especially when he was taken down so easily.

The sword never left his bedside. For a while, deep into the night, Gore considered the idea of seeking out Duke Marrok's room and slaying him in bed. But the smarter part of his brain not bathed in red reminded him that even if he could kill the Wicked Duke that easily, it was no doubt against Scadia's rules. He must meet Marrok in combat.

Provided, of course, someone else didn't beat him first. Sir Bobaunce, from the infirmary, informed Gore that the nobles had first crack at the scoundrel. If he beat them all then the fledgling knight was free to issue challenge.

The names of half-a-dozen challengers were placed beside Marrok's name on the board about the Great Hall hearth at sunrise the next morning. By evening Gore wasn't sure if he should be relieved or disturbed that the Wicked Duke had vanquished them all.

None perished, though many were sore hurt. But all were dukes themselves. Gore refused to consider the fate of a stableboy who dared challenge a Wicked Duke he'd shown up in the face of a dragon.

But first he had to wait for Alain's challenge. Their skirmish was gratifyingly short, Alain obviously surprised by its conclusion. Doubly gratifying for Gore as he knew he would never have been able to tolerate Alain any further if Sir Bobaunce's mouthy senior squire had been the victor.

"Bad business, this is," Jack o' Japes said, startling Gore. The bard had slipped up beside him silently.

When Gore didn't reply, Jack continued, "I wit our nary-do-well Wicked Duke has his eye on the throne. If he defeats all challengers and then King Marhaus himself, then the Duke Marrok becomes King Marrok. Nobody should enjoy that, hence his being such a tremendous sword-target. 'Twould be a good time to get thee gone from Scadia, methinks."

Gore reckoned a Federal agent would enjoy nothing more than getting Gore on the Outside. There, Gore was instantly arrestable. "I plan to challenge him myself," he told the meddling minstrel.

"Zounds! After the thrashing, the rush-sweeping, the hindquarters pounding he smacked thee down with yesternight? Friend Will . . . "

Gore heard nothing more. He put his bandaged hand on his sword hilt to cry out his challenge.

He advanced as far as opening his mouth when another knight, dressed in blood red armor, slammed open the door and rode down the courtyard atop a red-armored roan horse. He bore a terrible-looking broadsword in his right hand, and mounted on his left arm was a triangular shield, almost as large as he, bearing the lion-bird creature called a gryphon ripping a knight in half with its oversized talons.

Everyone parted for him. The only sound was the clanking of the knight's iron plating.

The Red Knight dismounted and bowed to King Marhaus.

"Knight of the Red Gauntlet," the king said, "are thou privy to the challenges issued by Duke Marrok?"

The mysterious knight nodded once.

"Would thou wish to issue challenge thyself?"

Another single nod.

King Marhaus opened his hands in granted blessing.

The Red Knight wheeled around and swung his sword at the Wicked Duke even as Marrok unsheathed his own blade.

The fight was as intense and brief as a summer thunderstorm. The Wicked Duke never gained ground nor landed any square blows against the Red Knight, and indeed was backed nearly into the crowd, who laughingly pushed him forward again. At last the Duke was reduced to holding his sword in a defensive vertical simply in order to keep his head from being sliced off his shoulders; at last the blade itself was cleaved neatly in two, and the Wicked Duke kneeled with the Red Knight's blade at his neck.

"Thou art bested, Duke Marrok," King Marhaus bellowed in a battlefield voice that rang throughout the courtyard. "Thou must needs swear to get thou gone from fair Camelot, on pain of thy life if thy vow is forsaken."

The Wicked Duke rose and bowed, but his smoldering gaze lanced the king—and then, strangely, hurled a spear at Gore.

"I vow to leave Camelot and ne'er return," Marrok finally told the royal couple.

A whirlwind of activity followed that nearly left Gore dizzy again. The Duke and his own Progress made a great show of exiting, a business consuming the lion's share of an hour. When they were finally away, the Red Knight himself left, as taciturn as when he arrived.

The royal couple called for a wine-saturated dance-feast in which Jack o' Japes was only one of dozens of performers. At length, dinner was served amid the relieved laughter of men and women who sounded as if they'd been given a stay of execution in sight of the chopping block.

Gore drank and ate, but he did not dance and his mind wended its way back to Castle Dolorous. Marrok had gotten off lightly, he fumed. He still had no intention of letting his humiliation go unpunished.

In his anger he failed to notice that the Lady Melisounde was missing until Sir Bobaunce was able to come down to dinner and asked if anyone had seen her.

No one had. Gore was the first to guess the truth: the Wicked Duke had carried out another abduction.

He leaped at his chance, grabbing the sword he still wore at his waist and kneeling before Sir Bobaunce.

"Sire! Grant me leave to chase down the villain myself. At a word from my lord, I will kill the rogue and rescue the Lady Melisounde." He looked directly into Sir Bobaunce's tired eyes. "The honor of High Tower will be restored."

"Sir Bobaunce," the king said, "does thou accept this offer of quest?"

Gore knew the knight could not refuse; he owed Gore his life.

Sir Bobaunce let out a long groan which Gore was certain was only audible to him. "I so accept, my liege. And hear you well, Will Son of

Gore. Should you accomplish this perilous journey set before you, I shall ask our gracious liege lord to bestow upon thee the rights and services of knighthood.

"But take you heed, squire. Two great obstacles lay before thee in your quest: the Perilous Woods are all about the road, and you shall pass through the horrid land of Agravaine, home of the Evil Witch. There may be many other unforeseen perils awaiting which will challenge your mettle and moxie and determine if you are worthy to be called a knight."

Gore bowed to hide his smile. He had found his way to smash two birds with one catapult: to bag him both a Wicked Duke into a shallow grave and the Lady Melisounde into a sturdy bed.

He faced the royal couple. "At thy will, I shall take my leave of the court and rest myself for the challenges spread before me."

"Ah, no, Squire William," the king said. "Betake you hence to Sir Odoacer for a proper arming, and then to the Chapel. There will you spend a night in prayer and contemplation, in humble confession and begging divine favor and mercy, in preparation for your errand."

In full armor, complete with a new broadsword, Gore was led into the castle chapel where yon door smacked shut behind him. A single Gothic window of stained glass aimed a shaft of rainbow light down upon the altar.

Gore removed his sword, which he placed betwixt himself and the altar, lowered himself to his knees, bowed his head, and promptly fell asleep.

*H*IS HORSE TACKED WITH A POLISHED SADDLE FROM Camelot's own stables, and himself smartly outfitted with all the accoutrements necessary for a proper quest, Gore set out for the Castle Dolorous. He heard the cheering vaguely, but his memories superimposed the laughter the villagers had heaped on him not so long before, when he lost control of his horse on the way to the Black Tor.

The skies darkened as he rode. The chilly air smelled sweet with coming rain.

He considered what sorts of perils the trip itself might have for him. He tried reaching back into his shallow reservoir of Medieval literature but came up with nothing aside from a green giant who could survive having his head chopped off by one of King Arthur's knights.

Jack o' Japes' songs were a small guide. Thus far Gore had mostly heard English and French tunes. The English preferred stories about combat and feats of physical strength. The French leaned to love and romantic challenges.

Gore preferred the latter kind. He would get enough combat with Duke Marrok.

But while most people associated the Middle Ages and England hand in hand, there was far more to Europe than that little island and France. The Scandinavians were still afoot (or aship), the Germans were learning to be ruthlessly efficient, Italy was a set of squabbling kingdoms, Spain was balanced on a teetering edge of fighting and uneasy truces between

Europeans in the north and Moors in the south, and so on. There was also Eastern Europe, home of Good King Wenceslas, and Russia . . .

Gore shook his head. Speculating about what Scadia might throw at him was a narrow muddy path to madness. Better to ponder what he knew awaited him.

What if the Wicked Duke refused his challenge? There was no face for him to save if he bore no honor to begin with. But one way or another Gore refused to turn around empty-handed.

He considered a number of insults that might rile the Wicked Duke enough to draw him out.

And if the Duke did meet Gore's challenge? Marrok had one cheek on the throne by the time the silent Knight of the Red Gauntlet intervened. Gore had his own native strength combined with an almost berserker fury. But Duke Marrok had been combat trained for years, while Gore's entry into this world was barely a week old.

Gore decided he would cross that drawbridge when he came to it.

It was only after he brought himself out of his hours' worth of ruminations that he realized there was a distant figure behind him. It slowed when Gore slowed and sped up when Gore did. Wishing he had a rearview mirror, Gore discreetly leaned over his horse's flanks ostensibly to check his stirrups, and had no trouble recognizing the man.

Jack o' Japes was following him.

Gore's hands tightened on the reins until his knuckles were white, but he forced himself not to stop to challenge the itinerant bard. If Jack really was a Federal agent, he was already in position enough to make trouble as it was.

At the next convenient bend Gore took his horse into the tangled forest—the edge of the Perilous Woods, he realized. The horse groused and nickered, then whinnied a bit as the shadows began closing in, but stayed put. Jack rode on by.

Gore waited. He wanted to give Jack a good lead. But despite the fact that it was morning the sky was darkening until the shadowed outlines of the trees melted together. The chill breeze turned into a stiff and wet near-gale howling like banshees from the forest directly behind him. The wind lashed at the branches which then took out their anger on Gore. He—and his horse—both felt they'd better exit the woods soon or the trees would whip them to death.

Getting out was easier said than done. Aside from the lack of light, the woods seemed thicker than ere, full of thorns to catch at Gore's trousers and scratch his increasingly discontent horse. When they finally did break out into the road again it looked—different.

He couldn't tell how, exactly. Hadn't it bent right instead of left? Wasn't it a little wider? This path seemed barely wide enough for a cart. But he was sure he'd exited the Perilous Woods the same way he entered. It must've just been a trick of the light.

His stomach unwound a knot he didn't know it had when he at last saw a sign writ with CASTLE DOLOROUS.

But the sign was rocking back and forth in the wind. For a wild moment Gore wondered if maybe it was now pointing the wrong way . . . but there was only one road. Remembering the taverns he'd seen on the road to Camelot, Gore reasoned he would learn soon enough whether or not he journeyed the proper way.

The sky was nearly black now with storm clouds and the road narrowed further. Now the wind seemed to be shooting straight down the road from ahead of Gore as if channeled between the trees. After an hour's passage the road was so thin a desk could block it—and indeed, one did.

Granted, it was an extraordinarily large desk. Its wings extended into the woods. It was nearly as tall as Gore himself, and Gore was tall even for his own era, to say nothing of the Middle Ages.

He tried to ride around it and a peculiarly high voice called, "Ho there! You cannot pass, squire!"

This was no Black Knight guarding a bridge; no troll, no ogre, no dragon, no Perilous Woods banshee. The man wielded a stylus rather than a sword.

"You cannot pass!" the man, tall and lanky and wearing a toga, shouted again. "Not until you have filled out the paperwork and received approval from official channels!"

At least Gore thought it was a toga. It was pinned at the left shoulder and stretched down to his calves. But instead of being white it was a bright red with gold trim. On the front was a golden double-headed eagle, each head looking away from the other, with a stylus in its right talon and a scroll in its left. The man wore gold chains about his neck and soft leather boots encrusted with jewels.

Beside him was what Gore would have thought the fanciest mansion in all Scadia were it bigger than a tollbooth. Columns flanked the tiny arched doorway. Red slates created the roof. Inside Gore could see multi-colored, heavy on the gold, paintings and tile mosaics of stylized religious icons boasting halo-crowned heads.

Mirroring the eagle, the man clutched a stylus in one hand with a thick sheaf of papers in the other. He pounded the sheaf with his fist. "My name is Agathias Diatribos, Official Registrar of this district. You cannot just ride through here, you know! You must secure the proper legal permissions first. You may begin the process with me."

"I'm on my way to the Castle Dolorous," Gore told him, "and 'twas my understanding that Scadia offered freedom of travel anywhere one pleased."

The man—a bureaucrat, Gore realized, if an expensively dressed one—wrinkled his nose and then scowled down it at Gore. "Aye, I know what King Marhaus has declared. But he has no jurisdiction. This is the domain of the Basileus. He wields sovereignty both secular and spiritual over all these lands."

"The Basil who?"

"The emperor, knave! God's Representative on Earth, Born to the Purple, Ruler of the World and Time, Master of the Bosphorus . . . !"

Gore sneered. "Aren't you a little late? The Roman Empire is long dust and broken statues."

"A common error made by unlettered fools. It is true the Western Empire fell, but 'twas only a husk. The holy Emperor Constantine had moved the capital from Rome to Constantinople well ere the Germans conquered Italy."

Light dawned from one of Gore's crash history lessons. The eastern half of the Roman Empire, headquartered in Constantinople and controlling regions long held by Rome, including Greece and Egypt, survived Rome's fall by nearly a thousand years. It stuck in his memory because it was such an odd juxtaposition: an honest-to-goodness Roman Empire bumping against the kingdoms of Medieval Europe.

"The Byzantine Empire," Gore remembered.

Agathias scrunched his nose so hard it shrunk back into his face. "A name thrust upon us by barbarians. We are the true Roman Empire. And you are . . . ?" He held up the stylus and paper again.

Gore dutifully gave his name, announced himself in the service of Sir Bobaunce of High Tower, and declared his quest to free one Lady Melisounde from the clutches of the Wicked Duke.

The bureaucrat shook his head and fretted, "No, that will not do at all. Quite a frivolous exercise. We shall find you a much nobler quest if you are determined to so waste your time . . . Ah yes! Here is one most excellent: the search for Prester John, the so-called king of a faraway desert. Three years ago he sent a terribly impertinent letter to the Basileus declaring that this land had long since forgotten its true purpose, and must revert back to its original foundations or else be . . . "

"Let me pass," Gore snapped.

"Very well. Dismount and fill these papers out—can you sign your name?" He sat behind the desk and had to extend his arms upward to write. "These papers give notice of your intention to use this road. The next set here declares your intentions to travel through the realm of the Basileus. These will declare how long you intend to stay and to state your business—when you pass this way again you'll fill out a duplicate set explaining how long you actually remained and accounting for any discrepancies if you remained longer than your original declaration."

Gore's patience was already nearly at an end. "Then may I pass?"

"Then I post the papers to Nikos for approval—he handles the district's commercial affairs. Then pending his approval he will forward them to the Exarch, and if he approves them he will send them up to the Magister Officiorum . . . "

All at once Gore realized why anything twisted, labyrinthine, and impossibly bureaucratic was called Byzantine. Without a thought he unsheathed his sword and swung it at the little desk clerk.

The man blocked it with his stylus.

"Tsk tsk," he said. "Violence against an Imperial official will advance you nowhere but prison. These things must be done properly or they shall not be done at all."

Gore tried riding past the desk but Agathias blocked his way. For a bureaucrat he was quick, leaping hither and fro wherever Gore aimed his horse.

Gore contemplated the cathartic notion of using his blade to slice the paperwork like Alexander chopping the Gordian knot. But aside from his previous failure, another on-the-lam memory bubbled to the surface.

"The Basileus is not my sovereign," Gore told him. "Not since the fall of Constantinople to the kingdoms of Europe."

The bureaucrat started blubbering but Gore cut him off. "Zounds, haven't you heard? The Crusaders were on their way to the Holy Land but decided to have a little fun in Constantinople, and sacked the city in the meantime. They replaced the emperor with one of their own. Now stand aside!"

The man stumbled to his desk and sorted frantically through his papers, at which point Gore galloped forward and didn't stop to turn around till he was a good fifty yards away.

"Give my regards to Istanbul!" he shouted, twirling his hand.

"You'll pay for this!" the bureaucrat shouted back. "No one uses this road without paying the toll! The Evil Eye upon you, then!"

All in all, Gore had found fighting the dragon less taxing.

Within the next hour the sky opened up with its best attempt to deluge the world in a second Flood.

The woods on either side closed in so tightly Gore felt as if they were trying to convince him he rode into his own tomb. The sky blackened and shadows followed him every time he looked behind. He almost wished Jack o' Japes were with him, though there would barely be enough room now to ride side by side.

At one point Gore saw tantalizing lights and the broken outline of a crumbling castle. But the tease of dry shelter vanished as he approached.

He slogged on through the rain, through shockwaves of thunder, through lightning that blinded him but did little else to light his way. At some point in the day—or evening, or night, he couldn't rightly tell—he saw the shades of the ruined castle again.

But how could he be riding in circles? The road continued straight on for mile after mucking mile. Or was it curving with gentle deception?

When he passed the mirage castle the third time, seeing dancing lights from it until he was nearly on top of it, after which it disappeared into the fog again, it was on the opposite side of the road.

Then the road itself was blocked.

Gore shouted a curse to the sky but it was drowned out by lightless thunder. One would think that recreating the Middle Ages as they should have been would include road maintenance, but here was a stand of thorns stretching from one side to the other.

He slid off his shaking horse and hacked away. His blade bounced off the thorns as if they were made of iron themselves.

He chopped and chopped again with the same results, except now his arm was vibrating from the blows. A fourth try and the sword merely slipped away from the wet and adamant foliage.

It seemed Nature, or God, or whatever forces were at work here were telling Gore he was not worthy to continue his quest.

He mounted again and turned around, feeling completely beaten down for the first time he could remember.

This time when the castle appeared a mud-thick road opened a path through the hedge walls. Gore thought he caught lights inside but they disappeared whenever he looked at the bleak walls directly. Once he saw eyes peering at him from behind a fog-woven cowl and caught himself hoping it was only Jack o' Japes.

The moat was filled not with water but thorns like the ones that had just barred his way. The gate was open and a stale draft from the castle crawled its way to Gore's nose. He wondered why the Scadians, so resolute about appearances elsewhere, would let a perfectly good castle go to ruin.

But such rational thoughts deserted him when he crossed the draw-bridge, so desperate for shelter before he drowned in the saddle he didn't care what form his shelter took.

Then he was inside, and the castle swallowed him in blackness.

*I*LLUMINATION IN THE DARKNESS: A TORCH SEVERAL YARDS ahead of Gore lit itself a moment after he entered. Then another one just beyond, and another. A cold draft swept angrily at the torches but failed to extinguish them.

And then—another mirage?—he felt a burst of warmth for just an instant from the direction the torches would lead him.

At the conclusion of the dim processional was the larger, warmer light of a crackling fireplace. Silhouetted by the hearth was a bed, crudely fashioned but large enough to accommodate Gore's well-proportioned frame. The room was chilly except by the fire; there Gore was toasted into drowsiness, though when he stepped back a few paces the biting cold returned.

The next thing he knew he was laying on the bed, aware of the crunching down feathers filling the mattress, vaguely aware of his own hand pulling a woolen blanket over him. Silence—almost an imposed silence—claimed lordship over his mind. But when he dreamed, he dreamed of laughter.

Mocking laughter. Children in school who thought he was weird for spending all his time building robots. Later, bullies who taught him the hard way how to fight. His parents, while they were living, when he talked about going to college.

Every laugh laid a brick of stubborn and angry resolve.

Senator O'Smith, the laughter of a man drunk both with wine and his small power. Maybe the villagers' laughter was good natured when his horse escaped with him still in the saddle, but it stung regardless.

More laughter, unfamiliar, cackling. It still echoed through the castle when Gore shot out of bed.

He'd thought someone was in the room with him—but the figure was gone.

He lay back down but he seemed to have lost his eyelids. The draft came and went like slow laughter approaching invisibly from the hallways. The fire's shadows played along the stone walls, but were those other shadows melting out of the firelight?

Something electric touched his shoulder and Gore whirled around reaching for his sword in time to see a shadow disappearing into the wall. But for an instant . . . Gore shook his head, wondering if he had been drugged somehow or was going mad. It seemed as if the shadow had turned back and glowered at Gore before fleeing into the stone.

He jumped at the crash behind him, then cursed himself when he realized it was just a log falling in the hearth. The warmth crept around him again, found his eyelids, pulled them closed.

Gore awoke a second time to utter silence. Room-filling fog muffled even his own quickening breathing. He breathed it in as he might inhale water. He rose again, groggy as if he'd not slept for days, and rubbed his eyes. Other eyes watched him from the foot of the bed.

This time he did grab his sword and swing it at them—through them. It passed right through the center of three figures whose laughter echoed off the arcing blade. They floated around the bed to flank him but nothing Gore did to stop them was effective. His flesh passed through their ethereal substance.

Gore did not believe in ghosts. What remained of his rational mind insisted upon it. At best he allowed there might be quantum phenomena in the universe that would pass for a soul. Reverberations of the no-longer living existing in some other dimension.

He reminded himself of this as the center figure stared at Gore inches from his face.

Flesh-and-bone hand swiped through empty air and the ghost showed teeth. He touched Gore's forehead and an electric shock jarred Gore's skull and sent him reeling backwards.

He shouted and jumped out of bed uselessly swinging his sword while the specters sang a song composed more of cat howls than words. Ridiculously he jumped out of the way of one as it flew past him, and tripped over something that was not there when Gore looked down.

One ghost flung itself out a door while another disappeared into the wall. But before the third could escape Gore leaped for the ground toward it, swinging his sword just inches off the floor. It clanged against metal.

A small conical shape wobbled backward and the ghost's image flickered. If not for his sword Gore never would have seen it: a bullet-shaped robot with a smoky mirrored coating to reflect the stone around it. Mounted at its peak was a small swiveling concave dish which, Gore realized, projected a hologram of the now static-filled specter. One that could occasionally fire an electrical shock.

The Haunted Castle did its best to keep Gore awake long after its secret had been pried into the light. Wind rattled and howled desperately as if imprisoned by chains. Now and again a woman screamed from the floor. The fire repeatedly died and was reborn.

Gore laid his sword beneath his bed, crossed his arms, and doggedly closed his eyes.

But his sleep was light and troubled, filled with his personal ghosts of bullies and parents and state senators all swirling around him as if he was the center of a freakish blender of flesh. He was aware of three more white outlines surrounding him but refused to pay them heed.

Until one drove a sword into his right leg.

That got Gore's attention—and yanked a scream out of him—but nearly too late. The next blow was meant for his sword arm but raked his back instead as Gore tried rolling off the mattress. Another blade sliced into the back of his left leg and he did himself no favors by yanking tender flesh away from the metal.

But now he had retrieved his own sword.

Gore let every aggressive feeling he ever had, ever ounce of self-defense, boil to the surface. Pain channeled into his blood to form the red haze dripping over his eyes. Gore knew it had to be so or he would be finished—he might be finished now anyway.

Dead or not, he refused to let his attackers live to brag their tale.

The first chest level thrust drove hard into bone. The "ghost" dropped like a stone, apparently crushing its holographic emitter to reveal a man beneath the manipulated photons.

Somehow Gore remained on his feet, fed by the waves of fear he could sense in the men through their spectral images. They floated quickly away, not through the walls but the doors, formless limbs trying to pull down the torches to mask their escape. Some torches fell but stayed lit.

His legs throbbed and each throb spurted out more precious blood. Still he ran. Even though he was growing aware, as the world darkened, that they were gaining too much distance for him to catch them.

Then two of Gore's robot-created tormentors of earlier that night happened to pass the hallway and noticed the wailing fakers. They swept forward with arms outstretched and heads bobbing back and forth, though passing right through the attackers—

—Who had stopped in surprise just long enough for Gore to close the gap. The first looked down in surprise to see Gore's sword coming out from his heart. The second put up some resistance but Gore had not come this far only to fail. That one tried to flee with his throat opened but tumbled forward after a few steps.

Gore, at last, collapsed. The floor was slick with his blood. He tried to rise but his damaged legs refused his command. The frigid stone felt warmer and softer than any bed ever had.

And still, his sleep was unsettled. When his eyes opened once more the sun was weaving up and down in the sky as if undecided which way it wanted to go. Now it was bright, now the gray of dusk, now raining, never night. Sometimes Gore could see the moon, and Venus, the Morning Star. Once the cyclopean red eye of Mars watched him with more than passing interest.

There was a dull constant pain in his chest. After what seemed to be a few years he realized it was the pressure of a small but sturdy shoulder. One he was thrown over. The one who carried him had red hair tied into a single braid that covered her neck, and pale skin on the way to burning from the outdoors.

The fingers holding him in place were delicate but clenched him securely; they smelled of earth and loam, and there was dirt under the fingernails.

Then he was laying on a blanket on a packed-earth floor beside another bed more roughly-wrought than the one in the Haunted Castle. An old woman lay in it with a steel in her eyes that belied the rattling in her breathing. She didn't so much rise out of bed as float, as if invisible ghosts were pulling her up by her arms.

"The Witch of Agravaine greets thee, wayfarer," she hissed, then cackled. "Oh, he will be fine, child. He be the one I've waited for."

Another figure stepped into Gore's vision: the redhead who carried him. A young woman with pale blue, deep, skeptical eyes. Her simple shift and light dress—both green—were smudged with dirt and dark bloodstains. She brushed her hands together and put her hands on her hips.

"I can heal him, should he let me," she said. Her voice was as deep as her eyes, as rich as the best soil in Scadia, and as clear as a mountain-born stream. To Gore she said, "I can take the Evil Eye from thee as well, but that will cost thee a favor whene'er I ask."

"Fine," Gore muttered. "Who are you?"

"Igraine. This is my aunt, the Witch of Agravaine, exiled to the Perilous Woods by Camelot. And thou somehow, even with thy injuries, managed to kill thee three of the Wicked Duke's henchmen who lay in ambush within the Haunted Castle."

Gore's mind twinkled with understanding. The henchmen must have stayed behind in Camelot to tail anyone sent after Marrok. What better way to lull their prey into a false sense of security than make him think no threat in the castle was real?

The witch cackled again. "Thou art a boil on the butt of yon king, stranger. And twofold, it is thy destiny to face down the Wicked Duke. Camelot and Dolorous only once e'er agreed on anything, and it was to cast out old Margri to this wretched place. Naught I can do to avenge myself in my feeblehood—but thou, O angry one, thou will take my vengeance for me. If thou lives!"

Gore looked at Igraine and said without words, *Do what you must to make me survive.*

She pulled open the drawstrings of a leather bag. Then she was holding a vial to his nose that smelled of lavender, lilac, and carnations. First he felt as if his body were floating, then as if his soul—whatever that might be—floated above his body, watching Igraine tend his wounds.

He did not float alone. Surrounding him were all the faces from his recent nightmares and he swung an ethereal sword at them as they laughed. Now and again Igraine would grab one and hold it for him long enough for him to slash it open, at which point it would disappear.

When every torturing face was gone, Gore watched the rest of Igraine's stitching with detached fascination. He realized their exchange was not quite one way: for every memory she pulled, Gore felt bits and pieces of bitterness or great joy of her own. Now Gore knew that she loved her aunt but hated the Perilous Woods and would leave this ramshackle cottage once she no longer had to care for the old woman. Now he knew that she had the ambitions—and the skills—to be a knight as well as a doctor. Now he knew that she loved watching the stars at night, tracing their courses, staring at them endlessly with a telescope. Now he knew that she felt frustrated by the belief that she would never rise above the peasantry in Scadia because the Witch of Agravaine shared her blood.

Igraine did not just tie stitches; she tied their memories together, lightly but indelibly in a way he did not pretend to understand. But a whisper in his ear told him this was no artificial binding. They were meant to meet again, and this would ensure that they did.

Lastly she grabbed Gore's floating self and pulled him back down into his body. Pain returned. But not nearly so much as he expected.

She looked him up and down once with her pale eyes, rubbed her thumb against her chin, then declared him fit enough to survive to fight another day. Then she said she would be about in the woods gathering more herbs and roots for a poultice, and vanished from Gore's sight as if the air had swallowed her.

The old woman's grin was wicked as she lay back down in what he was sure would soon be her deathbed.

"I see thy days ahead as clearly as thou smell my foul breath, stranger," she told him. A bent finger pointed at him. "A terrible burden lies on thy road ahead. I see thee covered in red, and I see thou silenced. But this, unlike most men, be a destiny thou will forge thyself, in fire, in blood, in muscle, in treachery."

Gore said nothing. He believed in prophecy no more than he believed in ghosts, but the implications refused to leave him alone. Covered in red . . . blood. And what else could the silence be but death?

She handed him a necklace, a silver chain ending in a black gemstone holding a thousand silver sparkles within. "Put it on, wayfarer," she told him, and he did. "When thou find Prester John, old king and progenitor of this place—and thou will meet him, mark me—the gem wields magic built inside to protect thee from the dangers thou will face in his castle."

He didn't remember falling asleep, and the cottage was empty when he awoke. There was a hearty fire in the hearth, though, below a bubbling cauldron of beef stew. A clean bowl and spoon awaited him nearby on a crooked table. No one burst in to protest when he filled the bowl and ate, then again, and washed both down with a cup of mead.

His horse was tethered to a tree outside but neither Igraine nor the Witch of Agravaine were anywhere in sight. Nor were any clouds; the sun had reconquered its domain and lit a broad road toward the Castle Dolorous.

He felt scars stinging his legs and back, and the hand cut by the Wicked Duke, along with tight bandages on all those places. But it only now occurred to him that he was walking without trouble. His brain dangled the idea of magic in front of him but he shook off that foolish notion along with any other similar physical or metaphysical implications.

He might try to find an explanation later. For the nonce, he thanked the young and tough maiden fair and her tougher aunt out loud in case they were in earshot. Then Gore mounted his steed and accepted Nature's invitation to resume his quest.

*W*ITH THE SUN RETURNED TO ITS PROPER PLACE IN THE SKY, and the clouds having given up their quest to turn the world into a single ocean, heat hotter than any cold fusion tank flared through every nerve in his body.

His broadsword felt as light as balsa. His armor was no heavier than paper. Even his horse adopted a particularly swift and smug trot. Gore was spoiling for his fight with the Wicked Duke until even the spoils of victory were of less consequence.

The dragon corpse had vanished. Gore wondered if perhaps the Scadians in Duke Marrok's fief had buried it whole, but he doubted it. Most of its unimaginably expensive mechanical innards would have escaped any harm greater than short circuiting. They could be salvaged for the next beast. While Federal agents were unwelcome within the barony's secretive boundaries, Federal technicians might enjoy an open invitation.

Then the Castle Dolorous appeared once more, a rip in beauty, hardened pus welling up from Scadia's worst infection.

The men guarding the battlements were already amused by Gore's approach. They laughed and shouted taunts as he picked up the calling horn and blew out three notes in challenge.

Then the Lady Melisounde appeared on the battlements. Her hands went to the stone wall as she leaned forward to watch—so at least she had not been bound. The soldiers parted for her and their jeering gave way to leering.

Gore appreciated their appreciation for her staggering beauty, but vowed he would not gaze upon her radiant countenance again until the battle's end. To say she was a distraction was to say the core of the Earth was warm. Touching her fire with his eyes just once after Marrok exited the castle would without a doubt be lethal.

The Duke did not keep Gore waiting. The drawbridge creaked its way down like an immortal giant transformed by a curse to serve under the Duke's feet. Or hooves as the case may be, since the Wicked Duke rode a massive black steed—a Frisian, Gore remembered from his days of equine speculating—with painstaking care across the bridge, followed by a number of fancily-dressed livery men.

He smiled down at Gore, who had dismounted but held his horse's rein, circling Gore twice before he finally deigned to descend from the saddle. One of the stableboys held the Duke's horse while Marrok commanded the other to take Gore's.

"Feed and water and brush it," the Duke commanded the stableboy. "Never fear, good Sir William—I will have it cared for as smartly as 'twere my own." His toothy grin told Gore that the Duke reckoned in a few minutes the horse would indeed be his. "It is Sir William now, aye? They would ne'er send a stableboy to do a man's labor?"

Gore had been roiling for the fight since he first learned of Lady Melisounde's abduction and was in no spirits for sundry chatter. He pointed his sword at the Wicked Duke. "I challenge you to a duel, Duke Marrok. Take it or leave it."

Marrok lifted an eyebrow. "You and I are both men of the world, Goodman Will. We both know the true cause of your quest—the lady yonder who keenly watches us both. And yet, ne'er even knighted, what hope have you of her? She cannot be yours. She will not be yours. This fight is not yours. Turn from it now and no shame will attach to thee."

"I'm no knave," Gore told him.

He flicked his wrist in a deceptively small move that swung his broadsword about. Marrok jumped back quickly enough so that only his left sleeve was slit open.

His face blackened. "Your way, then, and your head on a stake when

I'm done!" He lunged blade first but Gore all but locked his legs and held his ground. He well knew that with only Marrok's men as witnesses, and with Marrok defending an indefensible crime even by Scadia's Code, only one man would leave this single-game tournament.

The certainty of the Wicked Duke's intentions brought the red haze over Gore's eyes and he let it. The blood-steaming rage was his only hope of survival.

Gore hardly noticed that it was a sword he held. It might as well have been his own claws striking out at the Duke. No ground lay beneath him; the air cushioned his every move. In seconds he no longer even saw the Duke's face but only a black abyss where the head was and waiting impatiently to claim its bastard child.

The granite monolith that was Gore moved forward inexorably, a small step at a time, blasting lightning at the Duke in the form of the broadsword. When the Duke's face at last reappeared it was filled with terrified surprise. Gore did not bask or revel in Marrok's fear, or indeed, feel anything at all, not even rage any longer. He kept thrusting the sword mercilessly, efficiently, opening up a cut here and there in Marrok's body, numb to even the sight of blood.

"Do you yield?" Gore asked quietly.

He noticed nonchalantly that he had opened up a long red line across each of the Wicked Duke's cheeks when the face disappeared—running away.

The haze began to fade but not Gore's purpose. He turned in the direction Marrok had run but then had his first hint of reborn emotion: cursing himself for a fool. Marrok was in his saddle and charging Gore with sword down, while Gore had let his own horse be led away by the Wicked Duke's poker faced stableboy.

He jumped out of the way and barely dodged the Duke's slash but was immediately aware of the horse circling for another pass. He braced himself for the next Medieval version of the strafing run, letting his energy well into a burst of flight as the flying sword missed him by inches.

The logical part of his brain urged him to break for the woods. But the part that knew the Lady Melisounde was probably still watching refused to let him be so badly humiliated a second time. He ran toward the castle.

The Wicked Duke exploded with a triumphant laugh—obviously he thought his prey was running for the drawbridge. Gore was not. Instead he ran for the edge of the moat and hurled himself on the ground.

He was betting everything on the obscure bit of knowledge: that a horse would do anything in its power not to ride over a human being. And that this horse would be smart enough to see the water ahead of it.

The Frisian was a beast of war and trained well enough to keep charging when its master commanded it so, but its own primal instincts surged to the surface at the last second. It stopped short of trampling Gore and instead bucked at its master's kicking. Duke Marrok sailed over Gore and into the moat, where his brightly gleaming armor dragged him under the water until the tips of his fingers had disappeared from sight.

"Good horse," Gore muttered.

He didn't rise immediately. With the red haze gone he realized his entire store of energy was nearly spent. Nevertheless, he made himself rise when he heard the politely appreciative clapping of the battlement soldiers. Once Gore was on his feet, though, they turned away from him to resume chatting up the Lady Melisounde.

He met no resistance crossing the drawbridge until yet another knight blocked the castle entrance.

"Who in Dante Alighieri's frozen damnation are you?" Gore shouted.

The knight bowed stiffly and removed his helmet to reveal a fluffy-haired young man of no more than twenty. "I hight Sir Bachelere, knave, adopted son of Duke Marrok. I would avenge my father's honor. Have at you!"

Gore knew at once he was a dead man. His own feet weighed only slightly less than a transorbital airliner. The strapping youth wielded his sword arcing through the air to take off Gore's head while Gore could only watch in bemused regard of the unfair world.

But Sir Bachelere stopped abruptly with the shattered remains of a flowerpot dripping off his head. Forty feet above him, the Lady Meli-sounde's hands were still open from dropping the object an instant prior.

The soldiers cheered her most heartily and lustily and declared her the queen of the courts of their hearts. This time Gore had no trouble whatsoever breaching the dark walls of Castle Dolorous.

He strode onto the battlements and the raucous cheering transformed back into polite clapping. The Lady Melisounde offered Gore her hand; he took it long enough to haul her into him and give her a right hearty kiss as his hand traced the velvet of her back until descending the convex curves betwixt her hips.

The soldiers groused and grumbled and kicked at handy pebbles, but Melisounde returned Gore's affectionate gesture. At last they parted, and she asked, "Has thou my favor?"

He pulled her velvet kerchief from his collar. "I guarded it as the greatest treasure, M'lady. But Camelot is a long journey hence. We must needs take to bed ere we attempt it."

Her flushed face turned mischievous. "I can only be the lady of a Duke, good Will. 'Tis a blessing and a duty both."

"The Wicked Duke is dead," Gore told her and all the soldiers in earshot. "Long live the Wicked Duke!"

A jaw-working sergeant approached him carefully. "Sire?"

"From this day forward I will be the Wicked Duke. And thou, M'lady Melisounde, are now a permanent residence of the Castle Dolorous."

She curtsied. "I am at my lord's command."

The sergeant looked dubious until Gore added, "And effective immediately, everyone serving the Castle Dolorous will receive a pay raise."

"Ah yes, very good, sire." The sergeant grinned and threw back his shoulders. "Good work if one can find it, hah! Especial with the Wicked Duke's other women, ay? If I don't overstep meself, M'lord. But, ah, but begging pardon, sire, much as I hate to shoot the crossbow bolt in me own foot, it might be good to bury the last Wicked Duke before thou take on such a great and noble responsibility."

Gore didn't see what burying Duke Marrok had to do with anything, unless the sergeant was superstitious. Nevertheless, it verily was bad form to leave a body rotting in your moat—or at least the bones, since Gore wagered the giant crocodiles had already dealt with the flesh.

The tombs were buried deep within the castle cellar, the doors of each vault shaped like gravestones and carved with the names of their occupants. Gore grew increasingly perturbed as he read the inscriptions: Sir Eustace, the Wicked Duke. Sir Palamon o' Shortshanks, the Wicked Duke. Sir Last—himself far from the final name in the marble roster.

Now Gore took the sergeant's warning: Wicked Dukes possessed an inordinately high casualty rate.

And he reckoned that before the week had ended Sir Bobaunce, and no doubt a small army, would ride to Castle Dolorous to retake the Lady Melisounde from the newest Wicked Duke's clutches. Given the circumstances he doubted they would be any more honorable in combat than Duke Marrok had been.

Many men quaver when death is near. The shadow of mortality turns them into shades of their formerly robust selves, if robust they were. Others consume their remaining hours with their taste and appetite magnified, washing down the threat of nonexistence with revelry.

Gore was of the latter variety. He would take no protest from the Lady Melisounde when he used her blouse for a pillow, though she broached none. The rest of her dress followed as bedding upon the crypt's rammed earth floor.

In this tournament the woman proved as ferocious as the man and both spurred on the other's ambitions for total conquest. In the tombs the bones rattled jealously and coughed dust at the blood-filled warmth invading their moldy sleep, but the living ignored them, pounding yet another hole into the earth.

Gore was able to enjoy his blissful reign as lord and master of his domain for three days before the axe fell.

The Sergeant-at-Arms, Hal o' Neck, brought the warning as Gore was recuperating from the latest afternoon bout with Melisounde, who continued calling him thou in public and other pleasant stirrings in private. Gore decided to let her sleep, the possible need for well-dropped flowerpots and testosterone surges notwithstanding.

Sergeant Hal had already made preparations for war: across the battlements were great black pots of substances Gore could only assume were tar and oil. He remembered reading once that in real history, oil had generally been much too expensive to waste on besiegers while tar was often spared for dumping on battering rams or siege towers or wherever else fire would do the maximum amount of damage. Other notions about their use in medieval warcraft were, over all, Victorian imaginings.

These pots, however, were very real and ready to put to lethal use. They could easily hold one hundred gallons each. They were raised up on ingenious cantilevered devices for ease in pouring. Beneath them were piles of logs ready for a-lighting.

As to the party itself—which prudently remained out of pouring range—it consisted of Sir Bobaunce as well as the Charlemagne bust that was King Marhaus, and a body of twenty armored men Gore recognized as the knight's own home guard. They looked eager, though harried— they would have to be to get here in a day-and-a-half, if you figured in the time it would have taken a speeding messenger loyal to Duke Marrok to gallop back to High Tower.

Once Sir Bobaunce saw Gore, he lifted the horn on the post at the edge of the road and blew three notes in challenge.

"Hearken all ye in the Castle Dolorous!" Sir Bobaunce shouted. "Be it known that Will Son of Gore is a villain, a varlet, a scoundrel, a serpent in knave's garb, who has run through the Code by stealing the mantle of the Wicked Duke not only ere winning a dukedom in the tourneys, but in sooth ere he even was granted knighthood by His Majesty King Marhaus! Due to his ignoble conduct ill befitting of e'en a Wicked Duke, I would ye further ken that His Majesty has granted us royal leave to dispense with the time-honored Scadian code of warfare and bring down your illegitimate rule by any methods we see fit!"

So that was that. Gore expected no less. In fact, it was pretty much exactly what he had anticipated.

"Sergeant Hal," said the new Wicked Duke, "order your men to give me three minutes and then lower the drawbridge."

By his sour look the otherwise stalwart soldier apparently found a large distasteful mass in his mouth which he was obliged to swallow. Yet swallow he did. "As thou command, sire," he said, then turned to his men. "You heard 'im. Beat your feet to it, lazy scamps!"

The drawbridge shook the castle walls as it descended. Gore didn't doubt that it would shake the whole building down to the crypt, where he would end up if he wasn't quite up to the task he'd set for himself. But he was in place as the bridge came down, and Sir Bobaunce's warriors charged the bridge with mighty shouts not quite in sync.

Half of them at any rate. As Gore had guessed, the other half, or at least a sizeable number, remained to bodyguard the king and Sir Bobaunce. A Wicked Duke might have men ambush-hiding in the woods, after all, or mayhaps even the Green Baron might decide to pounce.

When Gore had first entered the Castle Dolorous he wondered why the main corridor was so narrow and ill-lit and sloped upward before opening to wider rooms and hallways. But the more he accepted the siege's inevitability the more he realized the corridor's strategic value: there was no way for two men to fight side by side. It was the only way into the castle—the only way Bobaunce's men knew about, anyhow—and so the men were forced to fight Gore not only one at a time, but with their enemy on higher ground and hidden in the shadows.

He had also had the castle servants soak down the hallway with water and throw the Feasting Hall's rushes all about the stone. When they came not only would they be packed, they would have no sure footing.

Finally, Gore knew he was literally fighting for his life, again. That helped.

He must not let himself be lured into anything longer than swift skirmishes with each man or even his red-hazed fury would eventually tire. The first three men were struck with such vicious speed they barely saw the broadsword that aimed for their necks.

The fourth man was more cautious but that only slowed him down.

Soldiers five and six attempted to fight side by side, getting in each other's way so clumsily they nearly hacked themselves apart without Gore's help.

The seventh man acquired no good fortune from his numerical placement.

Now Gore was starting to wear down but did his best to keep the exhaustion from his face. Then he saw soldier eight: a wide-eyed Alain.

He wasn't certain how the tail-kicker managed to wrangle himself a knight's job, but the dangling sword betrayed the fact that Alain wasn't cut from a stiff enough cloth for the position.

"Do you want to live?" When Alain nodded, Gore told him, "Turn around", and sent him back down the hallway with a sword smack to the rear.

Then as he had hoped, but by no means counted on, soldiers eight through ten began to silently question the use of dying for their master, even for such a vaunted lady as Melisounde—whom they probably assumed to have no use for them anyway—and retreated.

In a fit of dangerous bravado Gore followed them as far as the castle entrance, waving his sword in wide circles and shouting at the top of his lungs, which made King Marhaus and Sir Bobaunce pull their horses back a few steps.

Sir Bobaunce was red-faced and spluttering, "This—this—you are no Wicked Duke, Son of Gore! You are the Rotten Duke, you are so wicked!"

Gore jabbed his sword toward his men on the battlements, which they rightly took as the signal to raise the drawbridge.

He was fuming as the bridge sealed him back inside. Not because he knew his erstwhile master would call for reinforcements. Not because he may have definitively wrecked his chances for any further advancement in Scadia—though he wasn't sure, aside from kinghood, how much farther up he could go.

No, he seethed now because he noticed a familiar face hanging back on the edge of the woods a few yards from the war party: Jack o' Japes.

He was certain the bard would take his leave of Scadia now and bring in the Federal authorities. How could he not? He had just witnessed Gore kill several more men to add to the charges he already faced for the death of Senator O'Smith. There was an even chance that even if the wounded laying in his castle received medical help now they might still die.

It was also probable that if Jack o' Japes was a halfway-decent tracker, he may have found the three mounds of freshly disturbed earth behind the Haunted Castle as well. By late 22nd-century North American standards this defined Gore as a serial killer.

He exhaled a single harsh huff as if he could blow out the irony from his lungs. He'd fled to Scadia because of one murder done in self-defense; now he'd committed several more. Whether they were self-defense was arguable by the dumbest Sophist, considering the soldiers arrived due to Gore's play at being another Paris of Troy with Lady Melisounde as his Helen.

He hadn't enjoyed killing those men. But he didn't entirely regret it either. Scadia had set the rules—and their loopholes. The king himself allowed Sir Bobaunce to declare no quarter. If Gore was willing to kill to save himself after engaging in some less-than-pure actions, King Marhaus and Sir Bobaunce were equally willing to send those men to their deaths to preserve their own pride and unbalanced sense of honor.

But whatever rationale he employed, the problem of Jack o' Japes remained. It was a problem Gore would deal with after nightfall.

The first thing Gore did after claiming Castle Dolorous—no, the second thing—was to survey every inch of it with the help of Sergeant Hal o' Neck and some parchment scrolls locked away in the Keep that revealed themselves to be blueprints. Gore traced all the standard elements from the keep to trapdoors, and secret passages—most of which led to the bedrooms of the maids-in-waiting.

What he was primarily looking for, should it become necessary, was a secret entrance and exit. Many castles had built them in as a means of escape should even the keep, the most solid and defensible section, be overrun. Gore found one.

The problem was that it opened into the moat. Which was filled with man-eating crocodiles.

But his trepidation steamed away in moments like water on a black-smith's forge. Crocodiles were far easier to deal with than armored snakes possessing over-inflated notions of honor.

Gore decided to wear as little armor as possible after watching Duke Marrok's bubbling conclusion. As it was he was leery about wearing a chest plate. But after training and fighting with a broadsword, often in full armor, his muscles were the largest and hardest they had ever been and they also made him a strong swimmer.

"Sergeant o'Neck," Gore ordered, "get me some chum."

"Get thou what, pal?"

"Chum—something to distract the crocodiles. A couple of those bodies thrown in the moat should do."

He shot through the secret entrance's grate and pulled himself out of the moat behind the castle almost before his body realized he was holding his breath. There were no enemy soldiers waiting here—they hadn't yet enough manpower for a proper encirclement—and made straight for the woods.

Gore had reasoned that Jack o' Japes was staying close to the woods to have ready a quick hiding place should needs be, and Gore thankfully added this to his list of correct guesses.

What he hadn't guessed was that Sir Bobaunce would be close by the trees too.

The knight had been muttering to himself or Gore might have never noticed him until it was too late. Too late being a relative term since Sir Bobaunce caught sight of Gore anyway.

His would've shouted but Gore had the drop on him. The first blow was a solid kick between Sir Bobaunce's legs that utterly silenced the beefy man. Gore followed this with a fist to the nose that reeled the knight backward and unconscious.

Now it was Jack o' Japes' turn, but he was just out of Gore's reach and chose to run before he could be silenced. He bolted into the woods and a heartbeat later was out of sight in the darkness, though Gore reckoned Jack's crashing through the brush could be heard all the way back in Agravaine.

Now and again Gore heard a thunk or a whap, followed by an "Ow!" or a "Zounds!" or "Odsbodkins!" and a slowing of his quarry's flight. Another moment later he realized Jack had, maybe out of fear of getting lost in the woods or going far out of help's range, turned back toward the castle.

For several more moments the forest was black and suffocating and thrashing at Gore and trying to swallow him. Some ancient, primal collective memory in the back of his brain he never knew was there resurfaced and whispered of demons and evil spirits and other creatures haunting the night woods. With every thorn and limb grabbing him he nearly believed it. Cold panic trickled into his spine but he fought it back; he didn't think the bard was so successful. As he closed on Jack he could hear heavy breathing along with the stumbling footfalls.

Then they were back out in open air and Gore made out Jack's silhouette in the thin light of a clouded crescent moon. Jack leaped ahead with a desperate burst of speed toward the looming megalith of the castle but Gore matched him.

Gore may have forgotten about the moat if he hadn't heard the splash of Jack tumbling in first.

Jack screamed but it was no scream of fear. Agony clenched the bard and refused to release him. Gore fell to his belly and pulled the wailing young man from the water to see that a sizeable portion of the bottom half of his left leg was razor-mangled—heartily chewed by a crocodile.

Gore pulled the dagger from his belt, the only weapon he dared carry into the water, and poised it over Jack o' Japes' vulnerable chest.

There the blade hovered.

And hovered still longer. Jack had gone silent, all attention on the weapon but not strong enough to fend it off.

Gore realized in an instant why he hesitated. He had once leaped to Sir Bobaunce's defense when the knight was injured and unarmed. And the knight was a trained warrior. Gore knew that Federal agents went to fight school, but doubted Jack's wild-eyed look of helplessness was feigned.

Gore realized he could not kill a man who was not immediately threatening his life.

He considered killing Jack as an act of mercy. But even in supposedly primitive Scadia the wound was not life threatening. A stitching and care against gangrene would be the only requirements.

At last, maybe noting Gore's crisis of conscience, Jack asked in barely a whisper, "Friend . . . Will, why do you want to kill me?"

Gore almost laughed. "You can't be that dense. If I let you live you'll haul me back Outside and lock me away. I won't go back Out. Not alive, anyway."

Jack did laugh, albeit through clenched teeth. "Zou . . . Good Lord, man, you think I'm a policeman? What bad spirits of devils or drink has thou gotten into?"

"A policeman or a Pete. And don't lie. I still have the knife."

"Aye, and well poised." Jack inhaled a deep breath as if it would be his last. The night air did smell and taste especially sweet; Gore had never noticed before.

Finally Jack told him, "I'm an anthropology grad student. From Bradley University in Peoria, Illinois. I came to Scadia with a fake ID because I'm studying it for my doctoral thesis. Will thou take me inside ere I bleed to death?"

*T*HE OTHERWISE CLUMSY BARD ENJOYED TWO SPOTS OF GOOD
fortune the remainder of the opening night of the siege: first, Gore
believed him. Or at least ordered his soldiers to keep a sharp eye on Jack
if he proved a liar.

Second, Sergeant Hal had watched the entire transaction from the
battlement and listened with a veteran's trained ears. He brought a
medical kit to Jack's side at once, and the sergeant's battle-trained
stitching delicately belied his massive frame and brutish mug.

Gore made free with the castle's stock of wine. He had little use for it
until the siege was lifted, but it was the closest thing he owned to anti-
septics and anesthesia. He wondered for a moment why if you were going
to recreate the Middle Ages not as they were but should have been, to the
point where you allowed modern plumbing, why not modern medicines
too? Then he remembered the name of the role he had taken over.

When the night was long in the tooth, Jack o' Japes seemed as well-off
as he could be for the nonce. He even sang a little tune (minus his lute)
for Sergeant Hal—about a brave soldier forced to fight a distant war and,
worse still, be separated from his lady fair.

Gore recognized the music. It was one of the songs Jack sang to the
Greenwood outlaws with details altered hither and yon. Gore had never
felt any separation pangs himself, but it did seem that Scadians were especially susceptible to them.

Finally Gore told Sergeant Hal to get some sleep, which made the sergeant bellow with laughter, and sat down next to Jack. "Why a bard?" he asked. He couldn't wrap his mind around the idea of staying in a lowly station—particularly one where your meals depended on the good graces of others.

"I don't plan to stay here for eternity, but no king or duke or knight will open up to a peasant, and I didn't want to spend the next few years working my way up the ladder. I realized that in Medieval society—or at least in the Scadian version thereof—the bard is the equivalent to a bartender or a psychiatrist. Especially when people have been drinking all night to my music." His eyes gleamed wickedly. "And the women here love musicians."

All rationales Gore could understand.

"Tell me all thou know about Scadia," Gore demanded.

"Then I shall enter the tale at the beginning, Friend Will, or what passes for one. When the government decided to parcel off land ere the so-called Economy of Abundance was kicked off good and proper two-score years ago, and get gone some of the good citizens from our increasingly vertical cities, Scadia was one of the first alternate communities. A wealthy prince of a fellow named John—such was all I could discover about him—secured land in Northern California through means legal—or mayhaps otherwise. The result was initially four kingdoms and six cities—the others were called Constantinople, Canterbury, Ravenna, Avignon, and Toledo—surrounded by miles of a perilous thorn forest. The Sick Pen War wrecked all the other cities but Constantinople—though I hear tell Toledo got what was coming to it. And over the years the society mutated beyond its founders' intentions . . . "

"As every society," Gore said.

"Now there's one lone kingdom, consolidated under the umbrella Barony of Scadia . . . "

"The Byzantine Emperor might argue that point."

"For certes. And the institutions thou have seen: the royal couple of Camelot, the Wicked Duke—I suspect thou also had a run-in with the Witch of Agravaine. Do I win a prize?"

"And I suspect the founders' intention didn't include lethal combat,"

Gore interrupted. "And since there's no iron mine here, and perhaps no Federal technicians to fix the robots, and a dozen other sources of modern amenities, some of these schizophrenic Scadians need to turn a blind eye to occasional contact with the Outside. We're not as isolated as the Scadians would like to pretend."

Jack shrugged. "So what if they do turn a blind eye, Friend Will? Can thou speak in sooth thou has ne'er committed the like?"

Since Gore knew the answer to that, particularly after years of dealing with politicians and energy companies, he had no answer for the minstrel.

"And as for forbearing lethal encounters . . . Aye, but did thou kill any man who was no soldier or had not attacked thee first? Those men chose their lives and their perils.

"For the remainder, would thou care for any wager that life here be worse than on the Outside? Good men and women on the bottom rung of the ladder all too often stay at the bottom and cannot even glimpse upward, much less climb. Here anyone can become a noble. None will go hungry, none need be cold, none need fear—short of wandering too far into the Perilous Woods—criminal acts upon their persons."

Gore remained silent.

Jack stretched and put his hands behind his head. "You think these folks be odd, Friend Will, but they be no moreso than those Outside. Thou must needs only adjust thy lens. I reckon for the nonce thou are still here and not back out There."

Of course Gore could not go back, but he would not tell Jack this. Still, if he could . . .

Jack could be a good friend indeed. If he had verily been the confidant of knights and the privy counselor of kings and queens, the hope of peasants and the companion of maidens, he might know the ins and outs of Scadian society—the Code—better than anyone else in the barony. A good friend indeed, Gore repeated to himself.

Gore started when he noticed a figure in the open doorway until he recognized Melisounde's familiar curves. She was smiling sweetly. "A word with thee, M'lord?"

She took his hand and led him to the bedchamber where she shut and bolted the door. Gore felt his exhaustion sieving away until she asked, "Why has thou not ridden out from the castle to challenge the invaders at our doorstep?"

"M'lady, would thou have me exit in darkness to challenge ten fresh knights when I am worn from dispatching the first half of their number?"

"Is it pleasant for thee for the king and my husband to be camped at a stone's throw from our home?"

"Will thou begrudge me sleep?" Gore nearly shouted in return. All at once Melisounde's sweet face had turned viperous and Gore wondered how he had violated the Code this time.

No, not the Code—a spoiled noblewoman's expectations.

Mayhaps this was never about Gore at all but one large, if quickly rendered, twisted passion play for Melisounde. Flirting—then courtly love—with the handsome new and rough-around-the-edges stranger. Then her abduction, with the stranger coming to fight for her, and letting herself be claimed as the stranger's prize . . . all the while knowing her husband—and even the king himself!—would come to her rescue. Then she would watch excitedly, even lustfully, while the stranger and her husband battled to the death over her.

Melisounde's face grew darker by the second as if to confirm his worst thoughts.

"Are thou a man or nay?" she demanded.

"I am the lord and master of this castle," he told her, "and I will conduct my part of this siege as I see fit."

For a half-second Gore expected her to cross her arms and stamp her foot as the opening act of a pout. Instead she jabbed her finger back toward the door. He then half-expected her to tell him to get out, but instead she asked him, "Is it thy plan to continue offering our castle's hospitality to that treacherous music-hacker? I trust him nor his bemusing words not and would thou no longer give him comfort in our walls."

For some reason that made Gore angrier than the demand to face certain death just beyond the drawbridge. "He was sore hurt by the dwarf dragons, M'lady. He is our guest while he heals. The Code forbids we toss him out on his ear." The last statement was a blind stab but succeeded in taking Melisounde aback.

Besides, Jack was potentially too useful to Gore to be dismissed. He also realized in a stark instant of clarity that he desired no more deaths on his hands. He had no wish to go down in Scadian history known as Gore the Bloody.

Suddenly he was tired. He wanted nothing more than to sleep and told Melisounde so. When he dropped into their bed, clothes and all, he expected Melisounde to storm off. Instead she lay beside him and slipped her hands almost languidly under her pillow as she often did after they made love. When a pillow was available, anyway.

"M'lord," she cooed, "will thou kill my husband?"

Gore had no desire to kill Sir Bobaunce—or, again, anyone else. Sir Bobaunce was arrogant, but that was no capital crime.

"I will offer him the chance to surrender," he told her. "I have no grievance against thy husband."

His arm whipped up reflexively to block the plunging knife he hadn't realized she held until he gripped her wrist inches from his throat. One savage twist of that wrist and the blade dropped; another and she tumbled out of the bed.

"Femme fatale!" he shouted at her. "Faithless, cold Morgan le Fay!" He heard the words as if someone else shouted them, then his own mind snapped back in place. He never in his wildest dreams would have expected doing this to her—though there had been one particular woman in Los Angeles who had enjoyed it, granted—but when he finally gave a boot to her backside it was every bit as gratifying as Alain had promised.

He dragged her to the battlements, where the soldiers looked aghast as if he'd just told them he would throw her into the moat. He ordered the wide-awake Sergeant Hal o' Neck, "Sergeant, return this termagant to her husband. And I warn thee, this Herculean task will no doubt require half-a-dozen of thy best well-armed men."

Gore felt Melisounde's icy glare on his back as he stormed back to his bedchamber.

His adrenaline rush must have disturbed his bedchamber ceiling, as it stared down at him for the remainder of the night. For a time his brain was itching that the suit of armor off in the corner of the room was staring at him as well. It took another moment before he realized he had never before seen a suit of armor in the bedchamber.

He jolted out of bed as a cloud bade farewell to the moon and the moon's pale reply illuminated the armor's red sheen.

Gore leaped for his sword at the same instant the Knight of the Red Gauntlet slashed open the mattress. The knight's second blow was blocked but strong enough to send Gore's broadsword flying and all but crack his arm bones straight up to the shoulder. At once Gore knew why even the Wicked Duke had so much trouble with this man—and that Gore himself had little chance against him even with the red haze filling his vision.

Except the red haze did not come.

Gore didn't want to bet this meant the Red Knight would spare him. He would bet that otherwise he was a dead man. The thought echoed in the ringing of steel as the knight kicked the broadsword out of Gore's hands.

It was only then Gore noticed the knight was dripping wet. So he must have come in through the secret entrance. But how had he known about it? And if he was strong enough to swim it in full armor . . . but Gore had already felt those muscles in the knight's first blow.

The knight hesitated as if waiting for his prey to go for the blade again. Instead Gore enjoyed a flash of remembrance: the knight had stopped short of killing Duke Marrok. He offered the Duke a chance to yield. Farther back, he had appeared after the former Wicked Duke challenged everyone, including the king, to a duel. So it seemed the Knight of the Red Gauntlet came—was summoned—whenever someone in Scadia got too big for his iron britches.

'Twas a hope Gore could latch upon. "Are thou here because I have grown too uppity for my place?" he asked.

The Red Knight nodded slowly and silently.

The words tasted a mix of ashes and pus in his mouth, but nevertheless Gore replied, "Then I surrender, good Sir Knight."

The Red Knight answered with a downward blow that would have cleaved Gore's skull had he not rolled out of the way a heartbeat prior.

The next thing Gore knew he was running through the castle with the Red Knight close at his heels. He expected King Marhaus and Sir Bobaunce would not lift the siege even with Melisounde returned anymore than the Achaeans would have sailed home from Troy if Helen had been given back to them. He had not expected—though should have, he knew—to be a continued target for assassination. Maybe he wouldn't have been except for the Lady le Fay being so wroth.

There was no time to ruminate on Hell's fury, however. He knew there would be no escaping the Red Knight one way or the other. He may as well stand and fight and go down like a man.

He worked his way up to the battlements and demanded a sword—Sergeant Hal o' Neck surrendered his own weapon, long and narrow and thin and light, meant for combat but not too heavy for extended marches. Perfectly balanced too, despite the occasional nick, though Gore was certain its near-perfection would avail him naught.

The Red Knight appeared seconds later and the sergeant commanded his men to leave. Gore wondered if this was another bit of the Code he learned too late: no help when the Knight of the Red Gauntlet came calling.

The sergeant bowed, said, "Sorry, sire" with what sounded like sincere regret—who knew when there would rise another Wicked Duke willing to offer a universal pay raise?—and then Gore was alone with his doom.

He blocked every blow and managed to hold onto his sword but was forced back at every strike. After a very short time his spine was against the wall.

The Red Knight, a killing specter betwixt the shadows of a vat of tar and the unyielding castle wall, with Gore's only escape a sixty-foot drop into a crocodile-filled moat, took his blade with both hands, pulled it behind his shoulder, and readied the fatal blow.

Gore decided to exercise the better part of valor. He cheated.

Before the Red Knight could finish his theatrical death stroke Gore leaped past him with sword ready, onto the battlements, one foot on a tar vat as he perched himself high above the moat. The knight swung downward and Gore leaped away in time for the sword to smash into one side of the vat's cantilevered woodwork.

The vat tipped and emptied its contents across the stone floor. Gore ran quickly enough to escape it; the Red Knight, secure in his combat supremacy, did not.

The knight had no more than turned around before the tar piled up to his calves and refused release. There may have been fury under that helm for all Gore knew, but his enemy never made a sound.

Gore knocked the blade from the knight's hand and his long steel overreached into the only passage the armor allowed: a sliver at the knight's throat. A broadsword would never have penetrated it; Sergeant Hal o' Neck's thin sword was a perfect fit.

Blood seeped from the wound. Blood that smoked. Blood carrying wires and microcircuitry.

*U*SING HIS OPPONENT'S SWORD, GORE MANAGED TO PRY THE shell of the Knight of the Red Gauntlet free of the tar before the waking eyes of dawn could reveal the trick to anyone below the battlements. On a calculated whim he dragged the knight to Jack o' Japes, who stared at both the robot and Gore with wonder.

"What can you tell me about this?" Gore asked.

Jack shrugged. "Naught but that he appears to challenge anyone who needs taking down a peg or ten. And he ne'er speaks, not e'en in victory. And he was ne'er ere beaten. I always knew I picked good company!"

"So everyone else knew the Knight of the Red Gauntlet was a robot but me."

The bard shook his head. "If they did, they ne'er spake it, in their cups or out."

Gore wielded a dagger to pry open the knight's chestplate. "There," he said, finding a small plastic square with a blinking red light. Gore switched two of the wires leading into the box, which made the light shut off, then carefully unscrewed the entire power assembly from the knight's chest.

"What's all this then?" Jack asked.

"Automatic trouble alert. If the robot is damaged or needs maintenance it transmits a signal to a Federal technician. I just sent out a new signal saying the computer diagnostic fixed the problem and all's well."

He plucked out another self-powered box. "And this receiver, I'll wager thou good Friend Jack, awaits signals from yonder King concerning who, where, and when to give combat."

He also plucked out the robot's little "nugget"—its cold fusion power supply—and pocketed it. One could ne'er foresee when extra energy may come in handy.

He rolled the signal box back and forth through his fingers as another plan formed in his mind. He had worried at the beginning of the siege about further personal advancement . . . now it appeared another loophole was opening a doorway he never would have considered ere today. With great gusto he began ripping the electronic mechanisms and the brain-drive out of the robot.

"Are thou mad?" Jack cried, drawing back as if he were next.

"How's your secret-keeping?"

"Plenty good, I wit, or none would entrust me with theirs."

"Then I have another for you." Gore tipped up the dagger to convey all its implications. He stuck the Red Knight's helmet on his own head and light dawned in the bard's eyes. A jester Jack o' Japes might be but he was no fool. Behind his understanding gleam stood the recognition that Gore could be as useful an acquaintance to him as he was to Gore.

"Thou'll be well cared for here until thou heal," Gore assured him once he had completely donned the plate mail. "One of us may find the other another day when chance allows."

The bard waved. "Fare thee well, Red Knight. May thou need never come hunting for poor Jack o' Japes, hah!"

The soldiers were back at their posts and lowered the drawbridge for the Knight of the Red Gauntlet as Gore approached with a heavy sack thrown over his shoulder. Instantly the men outside were alert, even the king. "Good Sir Knight!" King Marhaus shouted. "Has thou dispensed of the varlet?"

The Red Knight nodded once, slowly, and tossed the bag of bug-ridden flour into the moat.

"Oho, and disposed as well as dispensed! Very good indeed!" Gore caught sight of Melisounde standing at Sir Bobaunce's side. Both laughed maliciously, though his former master's cackling was pale compared to the lady's.

Gore felt no pangs of separation from her as he strode toward the Red Knight's horse, a thoroughly roan animal he first saw back at Camelot. He bowed once to the king, pointedly ignoring Sir Bobaunce and Lady Melisounde, and rode off.

But where would he go now? The answer had been obvious as soon as Gore put on the armor: The Perilous Woods. Eyewitnesses had seen the Red Knight emerge from there, so into them Gore would wander. He wasn't sure what he would find—maybe nothing more than a stable and maintenance shack.

But one thing he knew about the Scadians was they were loath to do aught halfway. Gore wouldn't shed a nanobit's worth of surprise to find a Castle Perilous deep in the Perilous Woods.

Thus remained only the matter of the Wasteland.

If there was a Wasteland. It may have just been a myth, a bogeyman, a moot folktale to keep unruly peasants in line. Then again, he once believed the like about the dragon, too.

Once again Gore refused to bet too heavily on ease. If the Scadians said there was a Wasteland beyond their boundaries then he would almost certainly find one.

Not all the globe was blessed with weather modification. In fact, the environmentalists had long ere seen to it that many parts were unaltered in order to preserve their pseudo-pristine native habitats. In other places, modifications created detrimental effects on bordering lands. Chances were if he strayed too far beyond the pale he would land himself in the desert.

As he rode he passed the ramshackle cottage of the Witch of Agravaine. It was shrouded beneath a darkness that had obviously waited long to devour it; alongside the hungry black, the windows were boarded up. Gore refused to consider the metaphysical implications of this any more than he had those attached to her ambiguous prophecies.

And yet . . . her prophecies had come to pass. Gore was indeed covered in red and he had been silenced. After all, he wore the Red Knight's armor, and the knight never spoke.

Maybe there was something to the idea of destiny after all. If that be so, though, Gore would be certain to carve out his own in this place where it was easier to shape one's fate than anywhere else he had ever known.

His thoughts were interrupted by a woman's scream, followed by angry pleas to release her.

Weren't their rules here against coercion? Not that the Wicked Duke adhered to any. Gore spurred his horse forward to the tumult and saw a circle of men in Lincoln green surrounding a lady Gore recognized as the redheaded Igraine, the witch's niece and apprentice. Two of the Green Baron's outlaws held her by the arms while Robert o' Hardtooth laughed with his hands planted on his hips.

He stopped laughing when he bespied the Knight of the Red Gauntlet approaching. Though Gore was sorely outnumbered and knew it, the rest of the bandits backed away.

Apprehension and rebellion mixed in the Green Baron's eyes. "Were thou called for me, Sir Knight?"

Gore withdrew his blade and pointed it at Agravaine. "Leave her be, and I will leave ye in peace," he spoke without thinking. But no matter. Igraine had treated him more than kindly and he meant to repay the favor.

"Hah! We should ne'er know peace. But men who lust after it overmuch grow soft around the bellies, ay?"

Robert o' Hardtooth's gaze narrowed and he stepped boldly toward Gore. "I wit I heard thy voice ere now, Sir Knight of the Red Gauntlet. Verily 'tis a speech with which I forced myself to be most familiar."

Gore froze, glad for the helm hiding his expression. Was the jig up already? Even if he were in prime undamaged condition he wouldn't want to battle all of the outlaws.

Once more he discovered how tired he was of killing. He had hoped becoming the Red Knight would mean backing away and granting mercy.

The Green Baron stroked his goatee. Gore had a wild thought of kicking him aside and galloping off—but then the Red Knight's reputation would be ruined. He would be more than useless to Gore; he would become a target.

"Aye, I have heard thy voice indeed," the Baron told him quietly. "An' certes I recall the man who possessed it did spare my life when he may easily have stolen it to salvage his own skin. E'en in the Greenwood— mayhaps moreso—this means a great deal."

Robert o' Hardtooth stepped back and offered a bow half-mocking and half-polite. "Good Sir Knight, I release the Lady Igraine to thy custody. Deal with her gently."

The outlaws snickered as the Baron tossed him a pillion. "This be one favor, and in gratitude for thy mercy I'll grant thee two more. Should thou find thyself in need of aid, come to the Greenwood. Thou has the word of the Green Baron!"

He lifted his feathered cap, then he and his men dashed back into the forest.

Igraine stared at Gore with her head cocked to one side. She wasn't at all frightened, so Gore took that moment to lift his helm. "By chance, M'lady," he said, "does thou need a ride?"

"Thou owes me a favor for the cure of an Evil Eye upon thee, Goodman Will," she reminded him. "I would go into the Perilous Woods with thee."

"What makes thou believe I journey into the Perilous Woods?"

She stared at him as she might a child playing dumb.

"M'lady, it shall be as thou wish. And of thee I ask naught but good conversation. Thou are free to go and come as thou please."

"I did not need thou to tell me that," she said. "But I accept thy offer, good Sir Knight, and would welcome better than smallish chatter myself."

They rode. "How fares thy aunt?" Gore asked her.

"More peacefully in sleep than she did in life. She passed away to the next world the very night thou left as if fulfilling the last charge laid upon her. She rests behind her cottage, but I could no more stay there alone than a bird could spend her life entire on a limb."

"Thou had thy own destiny to seek out," Gore said.

"I wit I favor the direction of this conversation already, Sir Knight."

Gore heard a cocky reminder in the back of his mind that he favored redheads over blondes . . . but such was the old Wilson Gore, the older still Jason Caerwyn. Igraine was a lady not to be conquered but met mind to mind. Putting aside the thought of jumping into bed with her presented no challenge.

The odd connection he ere felt with her was resurfacing. Her mere presence filled him with a pleasure brighter and more filling than the best of his adventures in the sack with Melisounde.

The Perilous Woods passed quietly and without so much peril after all—though Gore still had the feeling of being watched. If the invisible denizens kept a keen eye on him, however, they must have judged him worthy to travel through unmolested.

"The creatures of the woods are amused," Igraine told him, looking slightly so herself. "For certes they never saw the Knight of the Red Gauntlet ere carry home a lady on pillion, or off."

"I am pleased I entertain them," Gore told her sourly.

"Be charitable, Friend Will. They let us pass, after all."

But Gore was less certain than she concerning their safe path. He owned to being poorly forest-trained, but it was difficult to miss the shadows slinking behind them not caused by the dappled sunlight, dark, low forms closing the spaces behind them like binding a fish while it still thought itself safe in the wide ocean. A twig-snap here, a bark-scrape there, and Gore felt the line of shadows behind become a flanking arc.

At last the forest gave way to a sun-drenched prairie, at the center of which was a small, bulky Castle Perilous. It was made of brown sandstone blocks and resembled an Arab fortress more than a European castle.

The drawbridge was down and, oddly, a plethora of plants hung from its battlements and towers. Gore crossed a little wooden bridge arcing over a stream to get to the drawbridge. Not far beyond were the brown mountains indicating desert a few hours' ride hence.

Conical robots with arms, wheels, and glowing embers for eyes were about in the fields tending a harvest of grains—for the horses, Gore realized. Another hammered at something in the stable, another groomed the roan horses, while more nurtured the hanging plants. They chirped and whistled at Gore as he and Igraine rode by. One even waved.

The castle itself was stocked with luxuries: plumbing served by running water, electric lights, thousands of books. The robots cleaned and scrubbed and beat carpets where appropriate. The pantry was stocked with fresh food.

The Castle Perilous also boasted a skeleton.

It lounged in a throne-like chair behind a desk surrounded by another dozen floor-to-ceiling shelves, wearing threadbare clothes more appropriate to an Angeleno businessman than a Scadian duke.

Whereas the library overflowed with history, art, and literature, these books concerned themselves with every imaginable discipline of science. The lion's share belonged to robotics.

"Who was he?" Igraine asked.

Gore examined the body. There was no sign of violence; based on that and the white beard still clinging to the bony jaw, he imagined the man simply died of old age. Igraine said something about burial, and Gore agreed.

The skeleton's right arm was outstretched to his desk, holding a long-dry stylus. Beneath the pen rested a half-finished letter admonishing the king and queen of Camelot that they had let the original principles of Scadia go too far astray from the founders' intentions.

Thus did Gore realize he had inadvertently completed another quest: the discovery of the location of Prester John. The builder of the Red Knight. The man who established Scadia forty years before.

A small picture on the desk startled him. Igraine . . . no, a woman much with her countenance but slightly older. The Witch of Agravaine, then. Gore wondered if her relationship to Prester John—whatever that had been—was the true reason she had been exiled to the Perilous Woods.

His thoughts were interrupted by a maintenance robot pushing him aside to dust the skeleton.

When it was done, Gore and Igraine carried the frail remains outside in a tautly-pulled blanket to see dozens of figures approaching from the treeline. The shadows had transformed into a myriad of bizarre shapes, all eyes shining through the sunlight as they fixed on Gore, who was still in the red armor.

The denizens of the Perilous Woods had come calling.

Every dream and nightmare of medieval fantasy appeared for Gore's consideration as if the trees themselves were transforming into the creatures one by one. Several surprisingly quick ogres had already made it to the bridge despite their dragging clubs. A griffin much like the one on Gore's new shield reared on its golden hind legs and flapped its white wings. Black wolves with yellow eyes and teeth ran for the flanking; various forms of legless things slithered in and out of the stream. Gray gargoyles with featureless eyes unperched from the trees to lumber behind the rest.

At last another dragon appeared—or the skeleton thereof. The iron frame was there and Gore noticed with professional, if morbid, interest the mix of hydraulics and muscle mass held within, along with the mixing bellows in the belly that created fire.

More robots unsettled Gore by following him and Igraine as they carried the body to the burial plot. His instincts told him trouble was brewing just swiftly enough to reach for a blade before the robots revealed their own shortswords, apparently lodged inside their backs. In only a few seconds two-dozen armed robots encircled them.

"Thou cannot fight them all, and I am unarmed," Igraine whispered. "What would they have of us?"

"You have moved the body of the Builder and stolen our guardian's armor," one robot answered.

"I can place them all home," Gore said. "But thy builder is dead."

They raised their swords and closed in.

"What of thy charm?" Igraine asked quickly.

"Methinks I will not speak my way out of this," Gore said an instant before he realized she meant the necklace her aunt had given him.

While he wondered how the "magic" was supposed to work, the gem warmed under the touch of his damp thumb and the silver sparkles began to glow. With sudden understanding Gore pointed the gem toward the robots and pressed it into its housing. The robots let out a single unified chirp and bowed.

Likewise, the forest creatures turned and left. All but the ogres, who began throwing rocks at one another.

"The sparkles are nanobits," Gore told Igraine. "Each one designed to post a cease-and-desist signal to any possible type of robot that might be in or find its way to Castle Perilous. Prester John must have given this to thy aunt so she could betake her way back here safely if she ever chose to."

"I ne'er once saw it till now," Igraine told him. "Why would she keep it hidden?"

"A secret unknown is a secret well kept," Gore said, mentally grumbling that he had not given the gem more serious investigation earlier. "Who controls it controls the robots—including the Red Knight and the dragons. Whoever holds this gem may keep in his palm the power to hold all of Scadia."

Meanwhile, the robots literally wheeled around to the corpse. They neatly broke off one finger bone—a holy relic?—and became mechanical pallbearers who buried their former master themselves.

Once done, the finger-breaking robot slipped it into its chest casing and popped a swiveling dish from its head. A hologram of a tall, lean robed man sporting a white beard hovered before Gore and Igraine.

"Greetings and salutations," the man—Gore guessed Prester John— told them. "I pray thou are a knight of good order and a lady of good stature, as I fear I must lay an impossible charge upon thee.

"If ye are traveled this far with my gem, then I must needs assume ye have also seen much of Scadia and ken our troubles. An ill south breeze blows through our fair land that may yet become a gale. Equality rots to servitude; displease a master and find thyself cast to the Perilous Woods or the Wasteland. No new souls are welcomed any longer. Hearty feasting and bold adventures are turned maliciously to blood feuds. My time to end this is past. I beg ye take this charge upon thy shoulders . . . "

"To change human nature?" Gore cut in. "Thou ask the impossible."

The specter lifted an eyebrow. "It is not so."

"So says any man who need not do the task himself."

Gore realized Igraine was a step behind him now, fearful but overwhelmed with curiosity. "I like naught pertaining to ghosts," she said.

"He's no ghost. He's electrons encased in a magnetic shell powered by a virtual brain programmed—taught—by the real flesh-and-blood man . . . "

"I am not unlearned in virtual reality and holoprojections, Goodman Will," Igraine said stiffly. "But I mislike golems. There be a whiff of hubris about them."

"More than a whiff, dear lady," the image of Prester John said. "Consider me no more than a library, then. One to consult at thy leisure, for I have neither brain nor spirit of mine own. The one who created me was greatly displeased at the thought of death ere his work was finished. When it be done, so shall I be."

"What thou ask . . ." Gore began.

"Is naught more than 'twas in the beginning. As to how the work is done—I leave that to ye, who must needs be a clever lord and lady, or ye should not have found thy way to this place."

The Red Knight bowed. "Wilson Gore of La Jolla, at thy service. My fair companion hight the Lady Igraine."

The whitebeard flashed a mischievous smile. "Aye, I ken her name, and it was she who bought half your passage through these woodlands and kept the robots so enchanted till ye moved my builder's body."

Ere he spoke more, the holodish retreated back into the robotic head from whence it appeared, and the machine itself made for the castle.

All at once Gore was exhausted and ravenous, and led the way back to the Castle Perilous. He put his arm around Igraine without a thought of seduction in his head. She gave his arm purchase to remain.

Illumination gilded his thoughts as he passed through the castle entrance, another portal opening: he had found a role in life which did much for him. In fact, it provided him with nearly everything he could ask for. He could satisfy his need for physical combat, work out his hostilities, and yet still be the defender of society. Of good.

Concealing his true identity under the red armor should be no problem, since the Federal technician would only come if the automatic signal sent out word of a problem. Gore intended to ensure that it would never send out such a signal.

Of course, there was one danger: Gore could be defeated, and so exposed. But a man couldn't have everything—even in Scadia.

This was followed by a further, more startling epiphany. Something he could never honestly have claimed, had never tried to claim, before his arrival at Scadia's wooded gates:

For the moment, Wilson Gore—or whoever he would be by the next sunrise—was a happy man.

Afterword

Tracy Knight

C LEARLY, THERE IS SOMETHING UTTERLY CORRECT ABOUT A
Knight providing an Afterword to this exceptional novella. But be
clear: I shan't be tilting at any windmills (of that you can be *certe*);
instead, I'll plunge my lance into the marshy ground so we can chat a
moment. Indulge me, if thou please.

It's just this: The existence of fiction signifies the *only* substantial difference between human beings and other life forms. Unlike non-human
Earthlings, we are equipped—even destined—to convey our dreams to a
neutral medium (paper being only one alternative), and to physically
hand our dreams to other humans, who then render their own adapta-
tions of our dreams. We do it every day, whether it's through writing a
poem or talking with our friends. It's astounding when you consider it
but, like so many gentle aspects of human existence, it's rarely cherished
or even discussed. Too bad, because it's right there. And right here.

PS Publishing's release of *The City Beyond Play* realizes the conveyed,
crisscross dreams of two men: Philip José Farmer and Danny Adams.
What dreams they are. For Phil, *The City Beyond Play* is a potent seed
wholly blossomed at last; the original, long-ago reverie lay dormant in
the Farmers' basement for more than three decades before reaching the
mature, robust shape it always deserved to fulfill. For Danny Adams,
the book realizes yet another important step in an exciting and promising
writing career, an exposition of talent finding voice. He not only lovingly
tends to Phil's reverie; he breathes his own unique life into it.

Born of a literary wormhole, *The City Beyond Play* ignores all strictures of space and time. The plot germinated decades before its completion, and the hundreds of miles between the co-authors was rendered both invisible and irrelevant. Astounding. This novella is truly a product of timelessness and folded space.

Like all of PJF's best fiction, this is a thrilling adventure, but it is much more: it is the universal human quest, the quest to *understand*. It's not enough that the main character vanquishes enemies or finds true love; what matters is the search for answers to fundamental questions: Where the hell am I? Why am I here? Who am I? How do I get through this? *The City Beyond Play* is an enchanting exploration of what Heidegger called our *thrownness*, the fact that we're all forevermore launched naked and ignorant into a story that's already unfolding. Like our hero Gore, we all are Outsiders finding our ways through strange lands, anchored by lingering pasts and vaguely promising but uncertain futures. We want what Gore wants: meaning, escape, and love. We want to know who created our Red Knights. We want to know where reality ends and play begins.

But as is true of the best of all fiction, the Big Questions do not dominate the story; they comfortably rest therein, smiling up at us. There is more than enough action, adventure, romance, social criticism and humor to keep us fully engaged and entertained. Moreover, the reader is trusted enough to read carefully constructed exposition, and at times to forego immediate action in order to sink more deeply into the physical and psychological environs of Scadia. There is much here to take pleasure in, and if you've enjoyed this novella as much as I have, I hope you'll reread it with the Big Questions in mind. By all rights, their exploration is one of life's best entertainments, too.

Philip José Farmer and Danny Adams bequeath the best gifts writers have to offer us: the exhilarating thrill of engagement in a tale well told, and a quiet substrate of meaning that sinks into us whether we like it or not. Ultimately, *The City Beyond Play* not only delights, it tells us about us.